Calling the Reaper

First Book of Purgatory

Jason Pere

Enjoy the chilling descent...

Jason Pere

ISBN-10: 0692744282
ISBN-13: 978-0692744284

First Edition July 2016

Jason Pere

https://www.facebook.com/jbp.author/

Acknowledgements

For Laura, My Valkyrie, that we may come to know a life without burden.

For My Family, Friends, and Supporters. Having an ample supply of willing spirits I was able to lean upon has made the journey far more enjoyable and much less frightening.

For Kat Hutson. Your critical eye and expertise with the technical face of the English language was a mighty boon for this piece.

And most of all, for those with fire in their spirit and steel in their heart, who take arms in the name of all that is good, the true Ladies and Lords of the realm, and those yet to be and to become.

Table of Contents

"In the beginning. In the time before. When the Unity sat atop the throne in Paradise and reigned over the world of man below, all was good and fruitful. There was life without end for every spirit drawing breath within the embrace of the Unity. Things were as such for a time longer than memory itself. But such things end. The day of the Shattering came upon us all. Paradise above and the realm of man below were forever changed. The Unity became no more, and from it was born both Life and Death. On that day, it was decreed that all who lived must one day die. And we the Valkyrie, the children of Paradise, became its warriors. Our robes were replaced with armor, and hands once empty now grasp sword and shield. Our charge is to watch over those who dwell below in the realm of man. We are tasked with the guardianship of every spirit that yet holds life. We shall protect them until that life is at an end. Then it must leave the realm of man. For each spirit that meets its end with virtue and courage, we the Valkyrie shall fly to them and bid them welcome into the warmth of Paradise. For each spirit that meets its end with fear and wickedness, they shall call the Reaper, and I shall mourn them as they are cast into the cold realm filled with weeping and the gnashing of teeth."

—Laurel, ArchValkyrie of the Thorn Crown

The Final Voyage of the *Sapphire Lady*

Part 1

She was a cruel and unforgiving mistress. Mood fickle and unpredictable, her fury was matched only by her passion. She had laid waste to all who tried to conquer her, all who stood in her path. She carried a proud magnificence, possessed of infinite beauty and allure. She captured men's hearts and watched them die as they were consumed by the cold depths of her being. She was the Cerulean Ocean, and Captain Dante Ramos was sworn to find her most hidden treasures. Then the debt would be paid, no matter the cost.

He had never fully acquired a mature comfort with the rocking of the sea. Beyond captaining a ship, he considered himself a swordsman, and no worthwhile swordsman cared for unsure footing. After all his years in command of the *Sapphire Lady,* he had learned to ignore the ebb and flow of the Cerulean beneath his heels. The Captain had taken the helm under the stars, as he was like to do on most clear nights. For all the discomfort he might feel at her touch, Dante loved to hear the vast array of songs the Cerulean had to offer. The breaking of waves against the *Sapphire Lady*'s bow, the wind whipping her sails to and fro as they snapped and cracked against the night sky, the muted chime of the ship's warning bell as she slowly shifted from port to starboard. Dante felt that the symphony of the depths was as engaging and moving as any music of man he had known. He had always loved meter and verse, the rhythm of a melody. He saw the raw beauty in all of it—the fast-paced fiddle and drum in a port town tavern, the robustness of the classical pieces played by the Queen's Capital Orchestra, or the resonate baritone voices of his own Cerulean Corsairs as they belted a shanty while setting sail.

It was a bittersweet fortune offered to him every time Dante's senses found the wondrous music of the world. It reminded him of what he owed, and of what he owed her. It was an impossible debt, he knew, but it would be paid in full. He would see his own body, every last man who sailed under his banner, and the *Sapphire Lady* herself resting in the cold fathoms of the Cerulean's arms before he ever surrendered the debt. No one could truly appreciate why he did what he did, though most spent their fair share of time wondering at the Captain's motives.

Captain Ramos and his Cerulean Corsairs had amassed enough wealth for each of them to lead a life which put most kings to shame. Yet every day, the *Sapphire Lady* set her course for another ship upon which to prey. It was not gold or jewels that Captain Ramos sought. It was merely freedom from guilt. Had it not been for his beloved sister Catalina, he would have lost all ability to enjoy the music filling his heart with admiration, would barely even understand the concept of music now. Had it not been for Catalina, Dante would have lived the rest of his life without sound, completely deaf.

When he was only a boy of six, Dante had been stricken with the Red Fever. The ailment was a cruel one to be sure. Very rarely was it fatal, but if left untreated, it crippled its victims by destroying their hearing forever. The treatment for Red Fever was well known and fully effective, and the critical herbal component a rarity. The plant known as Silver Bloom did not blossom freely in nature save in the most tropical climates, but under the skilled hands of a master botanist or apothecary, the plant could be cultivated and kept in bloom for sometimes even a month or more. The men of the Kingdom with the skill to grow Silver Bloom could easily be counted on a single hand and only serviced the lofty social circles of the aristocracy. For as common an affliction as the Red Fever was, the cure was only available to those of privilege, means, and standing.

Dante and Catalina were the children of a simple cloth merchant. When Dante's father discovered that his son had taken the fever, the man immediately resigned himself to raising a cripple. Catalina was not so pessimistic. She loved her little brother more than anything, and would see him conquer the Red Fever. Dante had been terrified as every day the fever's hold tightened and the sounds of the world around him began to fade away. The bustle of crowed streets and the busy market faded to a whisper. Catalina had stayed at his bedside every day to dab her brother's head with a cool cloth and hold his hand while he drifted in and out of consciousness.

Dante would never forget the night his sister returned home in the evening with an expression he had never seen on her features. In the third week of his battle against the Red Fever, his sister's face had lit up with a broad smile. But her eyes, those piercing blue eyes, had reflected a measure of deep sadness. She had rushed to Dante's bedside to press a small bottle into his hand. The fever had nearly finished its work on his hearing, but the boy strained to listen and understood he was to drink from the bottle. That bottle contained the Silver Bloom tonic. Somehow, a fifteen-year-old girl from a family of no renown had obtained one of the rarest medicines in all the Queen's lands.

Dante had always wanted to ask Catalina how she had acquired the means to save him from a world of silence. Each time he mustered the courage to inquire, he saw the pain veiled behind his sister's icy blue eyes, and his courage instantly vanished. Nine years later, Dante still wondered every day what cost his sister had paid to save him. The only difference now was that he could no longer ask her, even had he found the resolve to pose the question. Catalina had fallen ill with a sickness of her own, one that locked her in a perpetual state of sleep. His sister's condition was a mystery, and the healers a lowly cloth trader could afford were of no use. Dante became desperate to save his sister, by whatever means. It cut deep into his heart as he watched the days of her life wasted in sleep. Then those days turned into weeks and months, her youth fading more and more and spent without profit. Dante had known that, as he was then, he could never meet the task to find her the cure. So it was necessary that he become something else, something greater.

If Dante had learned one thing from the upbringing mediocrity had afforded him, it was that men only respected two things—money and prowess. He knew that the sort of money he needed to help Catalina was beyond his immediate grasp. In his heart, though, he believed that a man motivated by the purity of his cause could amass the sort of prowess which would turn others emerald green with envy. He counted the days until he was old enough, and at the first opportunity, he signed onto the Queen's Royal Navy as an Able Seamen. As Dante had hoped, even from within the aloof confines of her court, Queen Isabella had afforded him the measure of hope he had needed. He had to cling to it if he were to deliver his darling sister back into the arms of the living.

Dante soon felt as though he had entered a completely different world. He didn't mind the menial tasks the senior officers barked at him—tying knots, coiling rope, and swabbing decks. He viewed the orders as the cost of doing business, and he found his reward in the other requisites of sailing and soldiering. He absorbed all the knowledge of maritime tradition that he could. Any text on seamanship which fell into his hands, he read—vessels blueprints, maps and charts, accounts of ship-to-ship combat. It didn't matter the content; Dante consumed it veraciously. He was intrigued by the pistol, the musket, the dagger, and a bevy of nautical weaponry. Above all, he valued the saber. The Queen's Commander of the Royal Navy demanded that all who sailed for Her Majesty must be proficient in the tools of naval war craft. Dante could not settle for meager proficiency; he would accept no less than mastery of any weapon a sailor could use. He devoted every available moment away from his self-imposed academic studies to learning the art of fighting.

While his peers would spend their time with drink or women, Dante frequented the saber pell or the firing line, honing his warrior's acumen to a razor-sharp edge. After his first year of service, his growing comfort with his skill at arms led to competitions in the Royal Navy's Saber League. There he rapidly made a name for himself, winning match after match, and then tournament after tournament. His prowess with the iconic weapon of Her Majesty's Royal Navy gained him a level of notoriety among the Fleet Captains. The Navy's officers and commanders began to view Dante as a pretty feather to wear in their cap, and he turned their ambition to his own advantage. Within a paltry two years of enlistment, Dante had leveraged a Lieutenant's commission under Admiral Vega. The Admiral commanded the one flagship of the Royal Navy named after the late King's great-great-grandmother, the *Francesca*.

Dante had hoped that an officer's wage and his renown as a swordsman would loosen some heavy purse strings, opening the doors he needed for the proper care of his beloved Catalina. Sadly, the physicians and treatments to which he now had access were of little more help than those only the son of a cloth trader could afford. Dante still had not even been able to learn the name of the illness which locked his sister in sleep. The only common thread of each diagnosis was that the answers he sought lay only outside the

Queen's domain, if there was a cure to be found at all.

The news that his sister was beyond the help of any known medicine had broken Dante's heart, but he refused to surrender. Catalina had done whatever it took to help him triumph over the Red Fever, and he would return that kindness. He had thought that perhaps as a Captain of the Royal Navy, with the command of his own ship and crew, the opportunity to make greater allies and explore far and uncharted lands would now be open to him. He could find the cure. He petitioned again and again for his Captain's papers, and each time he was refused. It quickly became apparent that Admiral Vega wanted nothing more than to keep Dante within arm's reach, to boast at court of the Lieutenant's obedience. The powers that be would never accept him, born untouched by noble privilege, as an equal.

When Dante realized that the rank of Lieutenant would be the height of his career, he even asked to retire his commission and leave the Royal Navy. Again and again, all pure-intentioned avenues were closed to him. Then came the day when Dante's planning turned to plotting, and he began to conceive of a solution to his problem which required no honor whatsoever.

It took him six months of planning and two full years to set the pieces in place while he played the part of Admiral Vega's obediently trained hound. He bartered, bribed, and bought every favor and resource he could with his wages and reputation. He personally hand-picked a crew's worth of the finest sailors in Her Majesty's Royal Navy that he could trust. Over time, Dante saw to it that each man he had recruited to his cause was transferred or commissioned aboard the *Francesca*, and that her other crewmen were promoted or transferred to other vessels. Then, several of the *Francesca's* officers went missing, were met with unfortunate accidents, tragically killed in service, or discharged after some public scandal. And Dante was there to highly recommend his own hand-picked replacements to the *Francesca's* sudden and unexpected losses.

He would never forget the thrill burning in his fingertips as his plan had come to full realization. It was a mid-summer morning as the *Francesca* prepared to set sail from the Royal Navy's Harbor and into the open water of the Cerulean. Dante approached the Admiral and a handful of the ship's officers with the full force of his recruits assembled behind him. He informed the Admiral and what men remained loyal to him that they would not be making the voyage that day. They put Admiral Vega and a few of Her Majesty's loyal men ashore on a sandbar at the harbor's edge, and the mutiny was a bloodless success.

Dante would always think fondly of the looks of shock and disgust, the insults and threats the Admiral hurled at him as Dante's men struck the ship's colors and affixed her new flag. The name was painted over later, but that had been the maiden voyage of the *Sapphire Lady*, the first command of Captain Dante Ramos and the finest vessel to sail the Cerulean.

"Captain?" The voice of Dante's First Mate drew him back to the present.

"Yes, Mr. Ortaigo?" Captain Ramos remained still so as not to betray his reverie, but he wondered what would cause the unusual disturbance on a night like this.

"Our lookout spotted the lights of the *Star Bell*," Ortaigo said. "She is still on course, and it doesn't look like they spotted us."

"Excellent, Mr. Ortaigo. Let the crew know that we will take her at daybreak." Captain Ramos allowed himself a smile. His First Mate turned quickly and departed from the *Sapphire Lady*'s bridge.

The *Star Bell* was a frigate Dante and his Cerulean Corsairs had been trailing for nearly two weeks. Captain Ramos had paid a queen's ransom in jewels, gold, and other valuables to more than one information broker, wanting to know of her latest mission. He had learned that the frigate was returning from the far eastern seas and the Isles of Silk and Jade, thought to carry exotic spices and herbs. More importantly, he had paid for the news that among the cargo were rare items with possible curative properties, retrieved from the waters which lay towards the rising sun.

Dante dared briefly to think that, perhaps after years of false leads, searching, and sailing the *Sapphire Lady* across the Cerulean Ocean, he may finally lay hands on his sister's salvation. Perhaps the *Star Bell* had what he needed to deliver Catalina from the ever-sleep. Captain Dante Ramos longed for nothing more than to see his beloved sister open her eyes, those blue eyes which shone like two flawless sapphires.

Again and again, he thought of what he owed her as he sailed his ship beneath the star-lit sky. His thoughts consumed him like the inexorable tides of the Cerulean. At any cost, the debt would be paid. And then Dante would be free.

...and those who drink of the Praytos will see their nightmares made flesh and blood...

—Excerpt from the Book of Reaping

The Final Voyage of the *Sapphire Lady*

Part 2

"We're being boarded!" shouted the *Star Bell's* second mate. Those were the man's last words, for after the cry of warning, a Corsair's musket ball smashed into the man's jaw and sent him sprawling to the ship's deck. The crew of the *Star Bell* never noticed the other ship until it was too late. A cloud of thick, early morning fog had rolled in and concealed the *Sapphire Lady* until it was right on top of the smaller vessel.

Captain Dante Ramos had already cast his boarding hook when he heard the *Star Bell's* lookout call, "Blue Sail!"

Those were two words that every other sailor on the Cerulean dreaded. They meant that the *Sapphire Lady* was coming to call, and more importantly that Captain Dante Ramos and his Cerulean Corsairs were not far behind.

The *Sapphire Lady* was just too fast for them. Dante was admittedly surprised that a ship allegedly carrying such exotic cargo could be ridden down so easily. He had expected Queen Isabella to have ordered more protection for the frigate. Yet the Cerulean Corsairs set foot on the *Star Bell*'s deck before she could even order powder to her guns. It occurred to Dante that an exchange of cannon fire may have been more beneficial for his crew. The *Sapphire Lady* boasted at least twice the guns of the *Star Bell*, and the frigate was likely not equipped with anything larger than a twelve-pounder. Had they started with their canons before boarding, the Cerulean Corsairs would have sustained minimal casualties before boarding a ship hammered by two full rows of cannon.

Instead, Dante and his crew were about to engage the men of the *Star Bell* while their numbers were still at full strength. Dante figured it would matter little that the guns of the *Sapphire Lady* had not softened up the *Star Bell* for the taking. His Cerulean Corsairs were uncontested, the most lethal close-quarters combatants on the water. The combined weight of the trophies won by Captain Dante Ramos and his crew from saber tournaments could have easily sunk a small skiff.

Dante felt the jarring of timber meeting timber as the boarding hooks finished pulling the two vessels together. He now saw that there were more men on the deck of the *Star Bell* than he had anticipated, though the Cerulean Corsairs still outnumbered the Royal Navy Men aboard by a good twenty head. The Captain also noted that each of the Royal Navy Men he could see sported a musket, a brace of pistols, and a saber. That was a heavier armament than a typical Queen's Sailor carried. Clearly, what the *Star Bell* lacked in an arsenal, her crew made up for in personal weaponry. Perhaps the other ship would not be as simple to take after all.

The scattered and sporadic musket fire intensified. Soon, the only sound filling the sky above the water of the Cerulean was the rapid discharge of weapons being fired. Dante poked his head out from behind his cover on the upper deck by the helm. The fog was thick, and all he could see clearly were the bright orange flashes of muzzle flair perforating the silver blanket that enveloped the two ships. In terms of firearms, Dante had two loaded and ready muskets at his disposal, in addition to the two flintlocks tucked into the blue sash on his hips and the two holstered on his chest. Nearly all of the musket fire was exchanged over the ship's main deck, which gave the Captain two options. From his vantage point, he had a clear shot at a couple of unsuspecting targets; a few more men down would complete the siege that much faster. However, if he was spotted and drew too much attention to himself, it would make the boarding much harder than it needed to be.

The Navy Men of the *Star Bell* staunchly defended their ship. So far, the crew of the Queen's frigate had repelled each of the Corsairs who attempted to board the vessel. Combat had yet to transition from guns to blades. In the end, the Captain decided that a silent approach would afford him the greatest opportunity for an open foothold his crew could exploit. He pursed his lips in protest as he left one of his loaded and perfectly functional muskets at the *Sapphire Lady*'s helm, giving the upper deck of the *Star Bell* one last assessment.

He saw no movement on her helm. It seemed as though all hands had been called to the main deck. Dante griped the barrel of his second musket firmly in his left hand and quickly checked that his pistols and saber were snuggly sheathed. He marveled at the efficiency of his Corsairs' boarding hooks; The *Sapphire Lady* and the *Star Bell* were so tightly bound that the jump across was almost just a step.

Dante landed on the upper deck of the *Star Bell* quietly, his musket cocked and at the ready the moment his feet found solid purchase. He crouched low and made his way to the helm for a better assessment of the firefight on the deck below. It didn't take him long to formulate his plan of attack. The *Star Bell*'s entire crew, gathered on the main deck, had aligned along the ship's portside rail. It would be easy to sneak up behind them and show them what a real swordsman could do. The only threat to that plan was the potential for being caught in the crossfire of his own men's weapons. *Just stay low, man*, Dante thought.

Captain Ramos took the steps down to the main deck at a brisk clip. The fog was still thick enough that it was almost impossible to distinguish friend from foe. That was, until they were in range of his saber. He was not terribly concerned with alerting the *Star Bell*'s crew to his presence. They likely would assume he was another of the queen's loyal soldiers until he took aggressive action. He heard the splinter of wood as musket balls peppered the deck several feet away from him when he emerged on the far end of the Royal Navy battle line. The heavy, silver shroud of vapor still clouded most visibility, but he could readily see two sailors in front of him and the distant outline of a third before the fog swallowed the rest of the world. He took aim at the third target and fired his musket at the form in the fog. The man collapsed to the deck.

There was a brief moment of confusion as the two sailors took note of their comrade's death cry and the musket shot from an unexpected direction. That brief moment was quickly gone, but it was all the time the Captain required. Dante had dropped his musket and drawn his saber before the other two sailors were aware of their compatriot's final fall. He plunged the blade of his saber deep into the chest of the Navy Man nearest him and withdrew it from the corpse as the last sailor managed a glimpse of him. The final man of the three didn't even have time to draw his own weapon before the pirate Captain was upon him. The Navy Man managed to parry the Captain's thrust with the barrel of his musket, but Dante's second attack skillfully evaded the man's clumsy defense.

Dante pressed forward onto the main deck, crouching low along the ship's guardrail and keeping his head safe from any incoming Corsair musket fire. Another man quickly materialized out of the fog, and the Captain cut down the Queen's Sailor before the man could react. Dante wondered how long this sort of fortune would hold up. Could he really take the ship single-handedly without the crew even noticing his presence?

That fantasy was quickly dashed apart as two Navy Men rushed out of the folds of silver fog with sabers drawn. He tried to quickly dispatch the lead sailor to reduce the fight to one man, but his opponent managed to retreat from the first assault. The Captain danced with the two men, fighting defensively to stay out of harm's way. It was soon evident that these two swordsmen had little experience with coordinated combat; they pressed the Captain on his front instead of maneuvering to attack from multiple lines. With his superior grace and technique, The *Sapphire Lady*'s Captain forced his adversaries to all but trip over each other, and then he accomplished that, too. Both Navy Men went down in a heap at the Captain's feet, and with a few delicate twists of his wrist Dante made sure they would never rise again.

Shouting suddenly rose above the sound of musket fire. It was the nearby voice of Mr. Ortaigo. "The stern! The Captain's taken her stern! Over the side, now. You and you, follow me!" The First Mate's excitement broke through even the fog.

There was a rush of unintelligible words from both ships as the Cerulean Corsairs became aware of the opening before them, and the crew of the *Star Bell* realized that they were about to be overrun. Captain Dante Ramos then noticed the distinctive sound of boots meeting the deck behind him; his men had boarded the *Star Bell*. The sound of musket fire died and was soon replaced by the clash of sabers in combat. That sound comprised some of the sweetest music Dante had ever come to know and love.

The combat was quick and deadly. The frigate's deck was soaked with the blood of Royal Navy and Cerulean Corsair alike. Most of the sailors Dante faced were fairly skilled swordsmen, but none of them could truly match his level of expertise. The Captain of the *Sapphire Lady* was the driving force, the center of the melee engulfing the deck of the *Star Bell*. Men who recognized him fought to stay clear of his path, and most who engaged him were dealt with in no more than three maneuvers.

A man wearing a Lieutenant's coat emerged from the fog and came at Dante with a deep lunge. Dante made a low parry against the attack, but the Lieutenant feinted with a double-disengage to slip past Dante's guard. The Captain was a little shocked that he had not predicted the bluff but had no time to process the sensation. Reflexes took over, and Dante's feet were instantly in backward motion, retreating a safe distance. He refocused his attention on the Navy Man before him and approached with a ready guard.

He felt like he knew this man. They circled, testing each other with a series of light and noncommittal attacks. On a very shallow lunge, Dante finally got a good look at the lieutenant's face, and the memory flooded back to him. He couldn't remember the name, but he did know exactly where he had seen this other man before.

It had been the semi-finals of the Admiral's Invitational Saber contest during Dante's second year of service in the Royal Navy. It had been his first event in which most of the officers knew his name. There had been a large number of spectators, and most had even selected Dante as the favorite. He had fenced five other opponents that day, and each had presented a different challenge. But the semi-final bout had been the most difficult. The man he faced had only been an ensign at the time, but that double-disengage had scored four points in a row on Dante. He remembered the feeling of impending loss, like the match had begun to slip away, until he discovered a weakness in the man's third position guard. After that, Dante scored six points off the ensign's near shoulder, ending the bout with a score of fifteen to fourteen, and advancing him to the finals.

Dante pressed the third position, once again attacking the Lieutenant's near shoulder. The first attack was parried, as were the second and third. This served a measure of annoyance. *This miserable litter cur had the audacity to become a better swordsman since last I fought him,* Dante thought. The other man may have finally been a swordsman up to the task of offering real competition.

That was why Dante promptly drew and cocked the flintlock from his sash and shot the Lieutenant in the chest. The man fell over the side of the *Star Bell*, and Dante watched him strike the water of the Cerulean below. The waves of the ocean seemed jagged claws, pulling his body into the depths. Dante felt a slight sting of shame at what he had done, but he needed to win this day. He needed to win at any cost. And he was a pirate.

The Captain turned from the edge of the *Star Bell* and looked for the next man to fight. *Cortez*, he remembered as he waded back into the thick of the fight. *That was his name.*

The ring of sabers clashing and the crack of muskets and pistols firing eventually fell silent. The Cerulean Corsairs had taken the *Star Bell*. Captain Dante Ramos glanced over the deck of the ship at the floating bodies of the fallen. The Royal Navy had indeed fought to the last man.

"Mr. Ortaigo," the Captain called.

"Yes, Captain?" The first mate's voice came through the now thinning fog.

"See to the wounded and check the state of the craft. I'm headed below." The pirate Captain took the stairwell to the belly of the *Star Bell* and her precious cargo. The lower decks were just as he remembered Royal Navy warships—tight and functional. There was no room for anything which did not serve a purpose. The Captain prowled the ship with a flint lock loaded and ready, in case there were any survivors lurking about.

He found the door to the ship's modest cargo hold without issue, then braced himself before he breached it. Could a cure for his sister really be just one room away? Dante pushed the door open and stepped inside, ready to face whatever the room contained. But he was puzzled by what actually lay before him.

Where Dante had expected to see herbs, tonics, and medicinal powers form lands afar, all he saw was a peculiar little man sitting calmly atop a damaged gunpowder barrel. The man's skin had a golden-yellow tone, eyes narrow slits which housed a striking and even playful dark brown gaze. He had a long, thin moustache which trailed off into two black wisps, dangling at the sides of his mouth. Robes of dark red draped from his shoulders, stitched with small copper bows, and his dark, braided hair fell from under a matching copper-colored, square-cornered hat.

"Greetings to you." The little man's accent was just as foreign as his appearance. He rose from his seat and bowed to Dante.

"Greetings to you. I am Dante Ramos, Captain of the *Sapphire Lady*. May I have the pleasure of your name?" Dante asked. The Captain kept his flintlock in hand but lowered the weapon to a less threatening position.

"I am Motokumo Tomikashu, Master of the Imperial Gardens and personal herbalist and apothecary to the Most Divine Emperor Mako Tashanoshi the Ninth," said the man.

"Now would you kindly tell me where the ship's cargo is stowed?" Dante graced his question with an inquisitive grin.

"Certainly, Dante Ramos Samma, Captain of the *Sapphire Lady*. I and my personal possessions are the only cargo aboard this ship," Motokumo Tomikashu said with another deep bow. The man had some obvious trouble pronouncing Dante's name, but his effort was commendable.

"Are you not afraid? Death may be very close for you. I think it best that you not lie to me," Dante said.

"I do not fear death. I may be commanded by the Divine Emperor to end my life at any moment, and am at peace should my end draw near," the little man stated. "And I never lie. I have no skill with false speech." It was hard to tell from his expression whether he said this in jest or was just remarkably humble.

"I know there were medical supplies on this craft," Dante said. "I will have them." He searched the face of the other man as he spoke. Dante had known many liars, and only two things were clear to the Captain; this man was either telling the truth he believed, or he was the greatest liar of all time.

"You are correct, Dante Ramos Samma, Captain of the *Sapphire Lady*," Motokumo Tomikashu said. "I am possessed of what you seek."

"You are a healer?" Dante asked. His surprise warranted a raised eyebrow, and suddenly the matter took on a measure of clarity for the Captain.

"Yes. A healer is one of the many things I am," said the foreigner.

"Do you know of an illness that causes its victim to fall into unending sleep, even for years?"

"There is no such illness," Motokumo Tomikashu said. Dante's eyes fell to the floor; another false lead. "There is, however, a poison that will do such a thing."

Dante's heart leapt back up into his throat. "What poison? How do you know?"

"I know of this because I created this kind of poison. It is a lovely blend derived from the Lotus bloom of my homeland." Motokumo Tomikashu smiled.

"My sister suffers from this...poisoning," Dante said coldly, and his hand dropped automatically to the hilt of his saber. If this was the man who had created such a thing, Dante couldn't help but wonder if he had also been to the Queen's city, if he had anything to do with his sister's misfortune.

The man in the scarlet robes seemed to read Dante's thoughts. "I did not poison her, Captain Dante Ramos samma. I have never poisoned anyone. But I had many dealings with your Queen's Master Saboteur. Juan Dematiao samma has a fascination with my blends not meant to heal."

Dante had never met Juan Demataio face to face, but the man had a reputation as chilling as the *Sapphire Lady* and her Cerulean Corsairs. *What did Catalina do?* he thought with dread. "You created the poison," he said to the foreigner. "Is there a cure?"

"There is a treatment, and with the proper materials it would not take me long to turn the treatment into a full remedy," Motokumo Tomikashu said.

That was exactly what he needed to hear. Finally, his years of searching had produced a way to save his sister. Dante wanted to dance and cry all at once, but as a pirate, as Captain of the *Sapphire Lady*, he could not yet show his relief. "You will come with me, and you will treat my sister," he told the man. "I will provide any materials you request." He gestured for the healer to follow him from the cargo hold.

"It would be my honor," Motokumo Tomikashu said. "And that honor also binds me to another duty I must attend to first."

"Your duty can wait," Dante said. "My sister will not."

"I cannot refuse the call to treat the sick, and I will do as you command," the little man said with another bow. "But first I must plea to your sense of compassion." The healer tilted his head at Dante. "What do you know of the wellbeing of your Queen's son? Prince Raphael?"

Dante frowned. "Prince Raphael serves as a good will ambassador at King Duran's court in the west."

"Please forgive," the healer said, bowing his head low, "but I fear you have been deceived. Most have. Your Prince does not serve abroad. He has been sequestered within your Queen Isabella's castle, away from inquisitive eyes. Prince Raphael is deathly ill. In exchange for certain favors to the Most Divine Emperor Mako Tashanoshi the Ninth, I have been summoned to treat him."

"Treat my sister first, and then on my honor I will release you unharmed and you may attend to your duty." Dante couldn't believe the man was trying to argue with him.

"It is sad and not a simple thing. I will need no less than a fortnight to prepare the necessary remedy for your sister's condition," the healer said. Dante steeled himself. "Your Prince

Raphael does not have so much time. He may yet live only another four days."

There was silence for several seconds, punctured by the creaks and groans of the *Star Bell*'s hull as she swayed on the waves. The choice was clear to Dante. If this strange little man was all that he said he was, Catalina could be wakened from her bonds of sleep. The debt that Dante owed could be washed clean, but it would come at the cost of young Prince Raphael's life. Of course, he could allow Motokumo Tomikashu to treat the Prince before seeing to his sister, but even if the healer were to honor that agreement, there was no guarantee that the Queen's agents would allow a royal healer to resume dealings with a pirate Captain. There was no guarantee that he could safely move about the Queen's lands once Her Majesty's court got word of Captain Dante Ramos' return. Either choice demanded an innocent life, so why should he not choose that which profited him? The choice was clear.

The choice was so clear.

Dante looked long and hard at the healer before he spoke next. "You will come with me. I will see my sister sleep no longer." Just as he had sworn to do one day.

For Captain Dante Ramos, today would be that day.

...So it was that those who inhabited the world stood without end until the shattering. The coming of life and death brought with them the command of origin and finality. What had once been an ever-spanning memory of limitless promise became a finite series of moments, passing from one to the next. All that had and ever would begin would come to an end. And so, within the realm of man, placed between Paradise and Purgatory, time came to be...

—Excerpt from the Book of Life

The Final Voyage of the *Sapphire Lady*

Part 3

Not long now, and Catalina would be saved. The idea that he could cure his sister of the poison which had stolen nearly half her life gave Captain Dante Ramos an indescribable joy. Yet it was not enough to fully silence the echoes of his conscience; Catalina's salvation would likely cost the life of an innocent youth. To the Captain, though, the benefit outweighed the cost.

After the *Sapphire Lady* took the *Star Bell,* the Captain commanded his Corsairs to make haste for their home port. The *Sapphire Lady* could not find birth in the capital city's harbors. She was far too recognizable; her notoriety had made it difficult to do business ashore when the occasion called for it. Dante and his men were resourceful, though, and had circumvented any unwanted attention from the vigilant eyes of Queen Isabella's Navy.

There was a small cluster of islands to the south of the capital harbor. They were well secluded, and smugglers and other privateers often made use of them. The Royal Navy patrolled the waters surrounding the island, but its efforts were not concentrated wholly on the task. And there were many places to conceal a vessel there, even one as grand as the *Sapphire Lady*.

When Captain Dante Ramos needed to move about the capital city streets unnoticed, he anchored the *Sapphire Lady* within the sheltered cove of one of these islands. The Cerulean Corsairs had several ships at their disposal, anchored in hiding, and they often kept a small fishing craft or merchant vessel stowed discreetly within the hidden lagoons. Discovering the islands had served them well for many years, and they had conducted countless successful deals from right under Queen Isabella's finely powdered nose.

Captain Dante could see the secluded harbor now, and then the sea-worn fishing boat that would take them into the capital city. From there, it would be a fast and silent trip to where Dante had hidden his sister away—where he cared for her. He and Motokumo Tomikashu would stay by Catalina's side while Dante dispatched some men to acquire the necessary components for the healer's remedy. It was a sound plan. But like all sound plans, Dante knew it had to be seen through to completion before he could truly count it a success.

The Captain wondered how much he could trust this man. He had heard men say anything to save their own skins from the threat of death. Just because Motokumo Tomikashu believed his own words, Dante had no proof that the healer could actually perform the holistic feats he boasted. Still, there was nothing to lose in allowing the man to try. The healer from the Isles of Silk and Jade was thus far the most promising lead for a cure.

It suddenly dawned on him that this could really be it. What if this man actually saved Catalina? Then his mission was ended.

Dante had not allowed himself to think of what would come next. For years and years, all that had existed for the Captain of the *Sapphire Lady* was the next battle and the next prize. He had become so much a part of his own quest, his own lifestyle, that he never imagined he would one day no longer have his singular purpose. He would no longer have to be Dante Ramos, Captain of the *Sapphire Lady* and Commander of the Cerulean Corsairs. But then what kind of man would he become? He had only ever worn two other faces, and he did not have the heart to return to cloth trading. He no longer cared for the life of a Navy Man, even were he to find a way back into the Queen's good graces. Imagining what life looked like without his ship and crew was almost impossible. He rarely delighted in the more gruesome requisites of pirating, but no man could deny that Captain Dante Ramos was a formidable master of the sea, an expert pirate.

Perhaps the answer was much simpler. Everything Dante did, he had done for the sake of his sister, and soon they would be reunited. He could for the first time invest in being a brother. That was a remarkably pleasant notion, though he had no clue where to begin. He wondered if he would be able to find his way back.

He wondered who Catalina would be when she awoke. Would she remember the days before her sleep? Had she dreamt? Had she heard Dante speak to her from her bedside? He had far too many questions for her, and he tried to imagine the first thing she would want. Whatever it was, he would provide it for her. His sister could ask for the very crown on Queen Isabella's head, and Dante would offer it to her with a smile.

Dante imagined the sort of things brothers and sisters did together—attend the carnival, sing, dance, watch the geese swim in the royal pond. It seemed strange that a grown man and woman would enjoy the pastimes of children, but Catalina had only ever lived the life of a child. She now possessed the body of a woman, but she knew nothing of actually being one. Perhaps that was for the best.

The *Sapphire Lady* pulled alongside the fishing vessel and dropped anchor. Dante heard the calls of his crew as they prepared to lower the ship's longboat into the water. He left the helm and joined the men who would accompany him on the short row to the fishing craft. The foreign healer was among them, and Dante had felt no need to bind or restrain him. The man was obviously no fighter and posed no threat of escape. Dante also wished to engender as much good faith as he could with the other man, and the use of chains and manacles was highly ineffective for that.

The healer stumbled a little as they entered the longboat; it was plain to see the man had no feet for the movement of the water. Several of Dante's men chuckled when the little man tripped over his long robes, and Dante forced down a tiny smile. It was amusing to watch someone who was completely unaccustomed to the rocking of the sea, but he himself knew very well the discomfort. The snickers and sharp quips of his crewmen faded as they returned focus to their task, but the laughter reflected in their eyes.

Once the vessel made contact with the water's glassy surface, the Corsairs pushed off from the *Sapphire Lady*'s hull and lowered their oars. As they rowed, Motokumo Tomikashu turned an exquisite shade of green. The movement of the *Sapphire Lady* had seemed to give him some discomfort, so it must have taken all of the man's willpower not to lose his breakfast with the jouncing of the comparatively dwarfish longboat. Dante was grateful for the clear weather and calm waters; he couldn't afford an incapacitated healer.

The longboat reached the fishing vessel and Motokumo Tomikashu released a sigh of relief. It was an equally entertaining sight to see the healer leaving the longboat. Dante offered the man a helping hand, but even then the foreigner tumbled over the side to land in an undignified heap on the deck. Again Dante fought the urge to laugh as he helped the healer to his feet.

"Doff your colors before we set sail," he told his men. As recognizable as the *Sapphire Lady* was, the clothing of the Cerulean Corsairs stood out everywhere. Each of the *Sapphire Lady*'s crewmen wore deep blue coats and sashes. An eye-catching 'uniform' was an effective way to intimidate the crews aboard the

Sapphire Lady's prey, but it made it quite difficult to move through the portside towns without attracting the attention of the Royal Navy. So they stocked the holds of their smaller shore-bound vessels with common, nondescript garments.

They made their way below deck to rummage through the crates, donning clothing of simple browns and tans. In no time at all, the crew of the *Sapphire Lady* had transformed themselves from the Cerulean's most fearsome pirates to a handful of dusty fishermen.

Just as they set out for the harbor, Dante heard the warring cry from the upper deck. "Captain! Navy Man-O-War in sight!" Across the water, he saw several of his crew waive warning signals at him from the *Sapphire Lady*'s deck. Past his ship toward the mouth of the island harbor were not one but three Royal Navy Man-O-Wars, heading towards them.

"Back to the Lady, now!" Dante barked. He couldn't lose now. He was so close to saving his sister. Apparently there was one more fight in store for them before they could break free. It did not matter how many ships the Queen and her Admirals sent. Dante would blow from the water any vessel which came between him and his Catalina.

The crew pulled the anchor of the fishing ship and quickly made a return course to the *Sapphire Lady.* The cannons of the Man-O-Wars would be in range soon, and Dante hoped to stand aboard his ship before the fire fight broke out. He took out his spy glass and surveyed the lead ship. It was the *Isabella*, the craft which had replaced the Royal Navy's last flagship after Dante had turned it into the *Sapphire Lady*. That meant that Admiral Vega was among the fast-approaching fleet. But Dante had successfully evaded that old goat thus far; he was not about to surrender to him this close to the end. The *Isabella's* crew had finished loading powder to her guns, and the expectation of the sound of cannons blasting hung thick in the air.

The first round splashed into the water before the *Sapphire*

Lady. The next volley would likely strike her timber; there was not much time at all. Captain Ramos felt his mouth go sour as he watched helplessly from the helm of the fishing vessel. All three warships closed in on the *Sapphire Lady*, but Dante signaled his men to hold their fire. He wanted to make sure it was worthwhile if the *Lady* unloaded her guns. His ship was strong; she could take a volley from the Man-O-Wars before needing to return fire. Ship-to-ship combat was far less about firing first, and more about firing finest.

The next round fired, and Dante felt his breath stop as the flashes from the cannons faded and they waited for the inevitable crash of lead upon wood. The fishing boat finally reached the *Sapphire Lady*, and Dante was aboard before the hail of cannon fire rained down upon them. He would endure the Navy's onslaught beside his crew, where he belonged.

"Stay there and get below deck!" he called to Motokumo Tomikashu on the fishing boat. He would not risk the life of the man who could save his sister.

Dante gritted his teeth and kept his head low as he clutched the side of the *Sapphire Lady* for impact. The cannon balls rained down after ear-splitting bursts, but nothing connected with the *Sapphire Lady*'s hull. To a one, each shot completely missed, either striking the water around her or far overshooting her. Dante wondered what had possibly gone wrong for their attackers, but he couldn't waste time reflecting on the source of his good fortune.

"Return fire! Fire all!" he ordered. There was nothing but dreadful silence. No cannons were fired. "I said fire all!" he repeated. Nothing. He whirled to look at his men, and was met with the shameful eyes of his Cerulean Corsairs. In that moment Dante knew his fate had been sealed.

"You will not be making the voyage today," came the guttural voice of Admiral Vega as he emerged from below deck. The Admiral's face was set in the smuggest grin Dante had ever seen on a man. The Captain was slow to react as the full shock of the mutiny took hold. Several Corsairs closest to him darted in and restrained their former Captain, binding his hands behind his back as the Admiral loomed over him. "So, I have finally taken my ship back from you, you little thief."

Dante did not respond, would not give the admiral any satisfaction in his victory. It had the intended effect; his lack of response dug at the Admiral's pride. Dante let it go as long as he could, then turned his head and spoke to Mr. Ortaigo.

"What was your price?" he asked the man who had been his First Mate. Out of the corner of his eye, he caught the Admiral's distain at being dismissed.

"You made us all very rich men, Captain. But the Admiral has made us free men. A Queen's pardon for each of us." Mr. Ortaigo held his head up high, but his voice was laced with sadness. Dante nodded.

"You see? Your own men have taught you about the kind of loyalty you showed me. How does that feel?" Admiral Vega snorted. Dante said nothing. "You must feel like a fool," the Admiral continued. He was fishing for a reaction, but still Dante said nothing. Vega jabbed his finger into Dante's chest. "You thought you were so clever, so smart, you thieving cur. Now I'm the one who has outsmarted you."

Dante stopped himself from succumbing to both the Admiral's physical provocation and the attack on his pride. His silence would be his last act of defiance toward the Admiral, and he kept his face as unmoving as the ship's figurehead.

"Well, say something, you dog!" the Admiral growled. His eyes glared wildly down, and a lock of his hair had fallen out of its respective place. Dante only tilted his head to the side. "You were never even half the sailor men claimed you to be, you know. The legendary Captain Dante Ramos and his Cerulean Corsairs. No more than simple pirates and criminals." He bent and peered into Dante's face. "Speak, damn you!" he spat, and struck Dante in the jaw, splitting his lip. Dante only licked the blood away with a casual sigh. The Admiral's hands clenched into white fists. He reared back to strike again but then stopped himself.

"I am a gentleman, after all, and not without mercy," he said, smoothing the hair back into place. "I may yet spare your life of treason and piracy. Simply beg me for it."

Dante forced himself to look away from the Admiral and out into the ocean. The empty space grew between them, and so did the Admiral's anger.

"Put him on his knees," Vega commanded. The Corsairs holding their former Captain kicked Dante's legs out from beneath him, and he knelt on the deck of the *Sapphire Lady*. "I said beg me for your life, man!" the Admiral roared and finally could take no more of Dante's defiance. He drew the saber from his hip and plunged it deep into Dante's gut.

The Captain had won his final battle. He had known that Admiral Vega intended to take his time in Dante's slow and painful death. But the man had been so easy to goad into offering a quick end. For the Admiral's charity, Dante offered him a bright and flashy smile. Vega's face folded into a scowl, flushed with rage.

"Get this riffraff off my ship!" he bellowed, then stormed off the *Sapphire Lady*'s main deck.

Several Corsairs lifted Dante and without hesitation cast him over the side of the ship. The water of the Cerulean was cold—cold beyond cold. Dante had felt her icy grip before, but this time was different. He knew that, now, he would never leave her arms. As blood poured from the tear in his stomach and turned the sea around him into a murky red cloud, the chilling water of the ocean filled his lungs. His last thought was of his sister. *Catalina, how I have failed you.*

Then, in the darkest and coldest reaches of the deep, the Reaper came to collect the Captain. Soon, the *Harlot* would see her maiden voyage.

...A day shall come when a choice shall be made for all who keep fear in their spirit. Whether in deed, thought, or speech, it shall mark them guilty, and they shall be condemned for it. For the remainder of their days, they shall carry a heavy weight within. The guilty shall forever be beyond the warmth of Paradise, for a condemned spirit calls the Reaper swiftly...

—Excerpt from the Book of Reaping

Born of Titians

Part 1

Awake. Pain was the first thing Aristo felt upon returning to consciousness. The pain coursing throughout his entire body like molten bronze in his veins was all he could feel. Every part of him ached in a different way. His arms felt the sharp, stabbing pain of numerous deep cuts. His back and core felt the pulsing, throbbing pain of bruised and cracked bones. His legs felt the unreachable pain of torn muscles. His head and ears felt the loud, ringing pain of blows yet to be forgotten. Most of all, Aristo felt a new wordless pain in his eyes. The Praetorian was awake, but he saw only blackness. *Has the battle cost me my sight*? he thought. *Am I blind?*

As his mind returned to him and he grew accustomed to the feeling of total pain, he was able to register his eyes at greater length. He felt them move in every direction but still saw nothing. He then realized that only his eyelids were the root of the darkness assaulting his vision. The Praetorian willed them to open, but there was no result.

Aristo reached far within and blocked all the pain shooting through his being. *I am Praetorian, my flesh does my bidding.* Again, he commanded his eyes to open. When he finally managed to force them open, the agony consuming his head must have felt very much like staring straight into the blazes of the sun. He felt the tearing of skin as his world instantly turned from the darkest black to a moment of brightest white. His eyes watered heavily and he blinked, trying to clear away at least some of the dried blood which had sealed his eyes shut. For several moments, everything was a blur, but then he could distinguish colors and shapes again.

He nearly wished that he had in fact been blinded; he would have at least been spared the image before him. Aristo had been wounded in battle before, but never like this. His body lay covered in a blanket of dried crimson. No one would have known that he bore the deep purple uniform of the Praetorian Legion had they even bothered to look at him. It was confounding that he had bled so profusely and could still draw breath, still feel the beat of his heart within his chest. A moment of warrior's pride overtook him when he studied his twisted form and realized the excruciating pain was not unwarranted. Then he remembered.

Captured, he thought. *I've been captured.*

It had been a foolish decision, but then Commander Pullo was no sage. The idiot had ordered a mere three Decades of Praetorians to engage at least four, if not five, Centuries worth of the cursed barbarian savages. The Praetorians had only been ordered to scout and report enemy position, but Pullo was a well-known glory hound, eager to step out of the staggeringly vast shadow cast by his uncle's legendary tactical brilliance.

No Ballista, no Catapult, no Cavalry, not even a proper Archery Core, and the imbecile had ordered the men to break cover and fight. Pullo hadn't ordered any kind of flanking maneuver; he simply called for a full frontal assault in thick, wooded terrain. About the only thing that Commander Pullo had successfully ordered were the deaths of the thirty men who served under him. Pullo's brazen recklessness was a disgrace to his family and, now, all who bore the mark of the Praetorian Eagle.

Aristo hoped the Barbarian Rok had made Pullo's death a long and humiliating one. Despite their commander's gross incompetence, the Praetorians had fought bravely and with discipline, standing as a true testament to the Legion's honor. In the end, for each casualty the Praetorian scouting party had sustained, they had slain no less than four Rok. That was a margin of which any Legionary would be quite proud.

This was now the third day Aristo had been the Rok's prisoner. Or was it the fourth? He could not fully account for the passage of time since the battle. The beatings he received at the hands of the Rok Barbarians kept him unconscious and then foggy, and he had not seen the sun rise or set since being taken prisoner. The tent where they held Aristo captive was of crude construction, made of various animal hides sloppily stitched together. Still, it was quite large. Most of the foul instruments the Rok had used to torture Aristo were housed here as well.

The Praetorian mused that torture was an ill-suited term for what the Rok were doing to him. Torture was ultimately an interrogation tool, and that meant it was a means to gather information. The Rok were a bunch of slobbering, unshaven mongrels. Aristo had never heard one of the barbarians speak in the tongue of the Republic, and he doubted that the guttural grunts they spat back and forth could even be called a language. Whenever a Rok opened its mouth, all the Praetorian heard was the grinding of stones and the barking of sickly dogs. He was certain the Rok could not understand a word of proper language, so even were they capable of getting him to give up information, they most likely did not have the mind to understand it.

The Praetorian's thoughts darkened as he realized that, if information was not the reason for the Rok's continued cruelty, the beatings he received must serve some other purpose. Perhaps the Rok simply enjoyed being savage and cruel. Perhaps it was what brought them pleasure. He had done many savage and barbaric things himself as a Legionary, but he never remembered having felt any measure of joy form the darker realities of warfare.

The Praetorian allowed his eyes to soak in his surroundings. The tent was largely empty, considering how much room there was. There were a few large, wooden planks scattered throughout, driven into the frozen earth underneath. Aristo's hands were bound around one such plank, and the few Praetorians who had been taken alive with Aristo had been similarly restrained. But he saw none of his allies within the tent. All that remained of his fellow Legionaries were bloodied scraps of rope and cloth which dangled from the other planks in the tent.

Along the outskirts of the tent was a long and shoddily constructed rack, hosting a bevy of curved blades in varying lengths. Aristo looked at the fresher cuts on his arms and remembered each of the different blades which had pierced his flesh. The rack also contained coils of several different materials, rope and chain links for binding, and a few of leather. He remembered the unique sting he had felt as the Rok whipped his back and ribs with the knotted leather coils. Other devices were mounted to the rack, and these he had never seen before. He hoped he would never have to learn their function.

In the center of the tent was a smoldering fire brazier, from which protruded a handful of irons. The fire burning in the brazier was not meant to provide warmth, but only as a tool similarly used for the Rok's savagery. Aristo had not experienced it himself, but he recalled the screams of his comrades who had been held in the tent as hot irons pressed into their flesh. He cringed. This was no place for a warrior to die. Soldiers deserved a death on the battlefield.

Aristo heard the crashing of Rok footfalls and the jabbering of Rok voices. He was likely in for another round of abuse at the hands of his captors. The main flap of the tent abruptly parted and two of the mammoth barbarians entered, laughing and speaking in their gruff native tongue. Aristo noticed that the larger of the two had slung the limp form of a Praetorian over his shoulder. The massive barbarian threw the Legionary to the ground next to one of the planks and began to bind him again.

Aristo recognized the other Legionary; it was a younger man named Varus. He was appalled by Varus' condition. Aristo had not thought it possible for someone to be beaten, battered, and bloodied any worse than himself, but it looked as though Varus had proven him wrong. The most gruesome sight was the freshly mangled stump where the man's left hand had once been.

As the hulking Rok laughed and restrained the unconscious Varus, his smaller companion approached Aristo. The Rok standing before him may not have been the physical specimen of his comrade, but he was by no means a small man; definitely larger than any man Aristo had seen in the Republic. He suddenly remembered this Rok, the one who had done most of the torturing. He did not know the man's face, but he recognized instantly the telltale scent of rot on his breath and the stench of long-dried sweat and urine on the rags he wore.

This Rok wore a sash across his chest, made of beaten and cracked animal hide. There were several iron rings fastened to the sash, and from each ring hung an assortment of bones, dried and yellowed with age. Aristo had not given much thought to the garment before, but now it had seized his complete attention. From a ring fashioned high on the sash hung several recently severed fingers. Praetorian fingers. Varus' fingers.

This display of butchery struck something deep within Aristo. He swore on the name of his father, and his father's father, that he would see this Rok slain like the wretched beast he was. A floodgate had been opened within him, and his restraint and discipline were suddenly no more. He unleashed a barrage of insults and threats at the barbarians, but that only seemed to spur them on.

As the Rok laughed at their prisoner's outburst, the one adorned with his new trophies drew a hot iron brand from the brazier. Aristo cursed them for cowards and dammed the virtue of their mothers as the brutes took turns teasing him with the hot piece of metal. They waved the glowing iron close to Aristo's eyes and face, prolonging the anticipation of the pain soon to come. Then the Rok firmly pressed the flat head of the iron against Aristo's breast.

The pain was unreal, like nothing he'd ever felt before. Where he had howled in anger only moments ago, he now called out in agony. Only for a moment, the Rok withdrew the iron and let the man's skin char and crisp. The barbarians pointed and gawked at the blackened mark before renewing their attack upon the helpless Praetorian.

As the larger of the two took a turn with the branding iron, ramming it into Aristo's leg, the Legionary felt himself tap into a previously unknown realm of his spirit. It was as though the searing of the branding iron had awakened something long dormant and untouched. The burn of the iron turned into the chill of winter ice and wind. Soon, the pain was no more than a numb tingling. Aristo regained his mind and a measure of composure, and his cries of pain died.

He shouted in a voice filled with power and strength. "I am a Legionary of the Praetorian Republic. My father was a Legionary, and my mother bore three sons. My bones were a gift from Hrom the Earth Giant!" He felt a new sense of strength and determination flow through him, and he willed his hands to break free of the rope binding them. The Rok only pressed the hot iron to Aristo's body as he screamed at them.

"My heart beats with the might of Arin the Warchild! My eyes are made from Dia the Moon Caller's tears!" Aristo continued as he felt the ropes around his hands cut into his skin, and he struggled against them. The Rok realized quickly that their efforts no longer produced the customary results. The barbarians stopped laughing and now stood over him, puzzled by the man's rare defiance.

"My voice was crafted by Miraka the Siren!" the Praetorian boasted. He felt the blood flowing freely from new cuts as his bindings tore into him, refusing to release his hands. The Rok exchanged a few words before casting aside the branding iron and pulling a new one from the brazier. This new iron did not have a flat head like the last. This new iron ended in a finely pointed spike. The smaller Rok advanced on the bound Praetorian, and it was clear that the man planned to finish Aristo right there.

"My blood is filled by Ferrious the River Lord! My mind is carved from the mountain stone of Octunos the All-Knowing Father! I am Aristo, and I am born of Titians!" His voice filled the tent, and he felt the bones in his left wrist and thumb break under the force of his own will. Then he freed his hands and was on his feet at lightning speed before the Rok could ever strike with the iron.

In a stunned moment of disbelief, the Rok halted. That brief hesitation was all Aristo required. The Legionary fluidly relieved his enemy of the iron spike with his good hand and drove it into the Rok's left eye until he felt the point strike bone. The man gasped and convulsed, crumpling to the ground, and lay there dead. Aristo's other captor bellowed and grasped for the blade hanging at his side. But before he could manage to draw his weapon, Aristo struck him in the knee with the iron. The Rok went down to the sound of splintering bone. For a few brief moments the barbarian yelled in pain, then tried to shield himself with raised arms as Aristo mercilessly beat him with the iron. It took only a few blows, and after that there was no sound in the tent but Aristo's labored breathing.

He wondered if the cries of the dead would summon more barbarians to the tent. He resolved to kill as many as he could before being overwhelmed. But no one came. Aristo figured that the sounds of screaming and dying men in the tent were not a cause for alarm, that they were expected and would bring no one to investigate.

As the heat of the moment died, Aristo felt the pain returning. He commanded it to cease. He quickly surveyed the tent for provisions and tools of escape. He could at least arm himself, and Varus, but the tent offered little in the way of other supplies.

Kneeling beside Varus, he gently put a hand on his shoulder. "Wake, Brother." The other Praetorian groggily opened his eyes, then looked at the two Rok corpses and Aristo's blood-covered face. Then Varus' attention went slowly to the mutilated mass of flesh and bone where his left hand had once been.

"What are our orders now?" Varus rasped.

Aristo looked the other Praetorian directly in the eyes and spoke with firm resolve. "We bind our wounds, arm ourselves, and escape this camp. Then we return to bring the full force of the Legion down upon the Rok. We will make them suffer."

...For those in the realm of man, I giveth eternal shelter beneath my wings...

—Final line of the Valkyrie Creed

Born of Titians

Part 2

Aristo and Varus would not concede defeat, they would not surrender, they would not kneel down before death. In the face of overwhelming odds, they refused to yield; they were Praetorian. The two Legionaries had slipped out of the barbarian camp undetected. They had been able to quickly scavenge weapons and enough provisions to reach the last known position of their Century before disappearing into the frozen woodland. They had been on foot for two days, and it would be another four days before they would be clear of enemy territory, six if the weather turned on them. For now, the skies were clear, though the air was bitter and cold. The wind seemed to kick up arctic blades that sliced at the Praetorians' bare faces and forearms.

The journey had been grueling thus far. While the weather had been on their side, Aristo and Varus were not well-traveled in the lands of the Rok, unfamiliar with the best way to navigate the foreign terrain. They had only been able to secure very little food and fresh water rations from the camp, so they sustained themselves on the absolute minimum needed to survive. While they were fortunate enough to have scavenged some of their own weapons, armor, and shields from the barbarian stores, the weight of their armament was noticeably cumbersome for cross-country travel. The wounds they had suffered at the hands of the Rok torturers were certainly their greatest hindrance.

Aristo felt a great measure of pride mixed with pity whenever he happened to glance at the butchered stump of Varus's left wrist. Varus never complained about his injury; he was a finely disciplined soldier and an inspiration even as crippled he was. The red-stained bandages around the end of Varus's left arm were no longer soaked and dripping, so the fact that the bleeding had stopped was some small consolation.

More than the weight of their stores and the painful injuries they bore, the men spent their time thinking of other pressing matters. They knew their clumsy tracks would be easy enough to spot, and once the Rok realized what had happened, they would almost certainly dispatch pursuers. The Praetorians already felt hunted through the maze of tall trees and white, powder-covered earth. There was no sense in weighing probabilities. The Rok *would* catch up to them; it was just a matter of when. But they would stand their ground as though they were a full Legion Century, and they would show these savages another taste of Praetorian Republic honor and bravery. They would slay as many Rok as they could before being overtaken. Still, the brothers-in-arms clutched at the fleeting hope of reaching allied ground before having to fight their foe one more time.

"Let's have a look at that," Aristo said, gesturing to the wraps on Varus's left arm. The words came forced and on ragged breath, the cold air hanging heavy in his lungs. It was now midday, and they had just finished climbing a steep hill that had been more formidable than they expected.

"I can continue. I don't need to stop," Varus said stoically. The wounded Praetorian bit his lip as he caught himself looking too long at his left arm.

"I know you would continue to march until you reached the steps of the Republic Capital, but I need a few moments, Varus," Aristo lied. He knew the other man was proud and would not allow himself to be a burden to his fellow.

"I thought you would have a greater constitution," Varus jested with a partial smile.

"I can go as long as you can, Brother." Aristo matched the banter with a grin of his own. "This hill will give us a strong vantage point. It's likely the best place we will see to rest today. We should take food and drink."

"Very well. If you insist, we shall rest for a few moments," Varus said. The Legionaries doffed their packs and lay down their shields and spears while they looked for the least uncomfortable patch of cold, hard ground for sitting.

"Before we eat, let me see that scratch of yours." Aristo still wanted to offer care for his comrade but managed it better with nonchalance. Varus hesitantly offered his left arm, wincing minimally as Aristo undressed the bandage. "The color is good. It looks like the wound is still clean. The cold should help stay infection, and it is good the bleeding has stopped. It needs to stay dry to avoid gangrene."

"You have trained with the Medicus?" Varus asked. Aristo had never seen him show such curiosity.

"Not formally, no. But I spent many days as their subject and listened to the Medicus treating the Legionaries in the beds next to mine." He glanced at several of his long-healed battle scars. He completed the investigation of his friend's wound as gently as he could, careful to avoid touching any deeper cuts and keeping his probing to a minimum. Varus' face was stone throughout the inspection. He barely made a sound, and his face showed more annoyance than pain. When Aristo was satisfied, he turned the cloth bandage over and redressed the arm with the clean side.

Varus let out the deep breath, silently held for longer than Aristo had noticed. "That feels better. Thank you, Brother."

"It should be enough to get you through until we rejoin the rest of our Century. I will make sure you receive proper attention and immediate care. We have had enough of our brothers laid down on this battlefield."

They sat upon the larger rocks that peeked out from under the thin layer of snow. Aristo reached into his pack and withdrew a couple strips of dried meat and a small, half-empty water skin. They ate slowly, trying to create the illusion that there was more food than they truly had. Aristo found himself growing somewhat fond of the taste; the meat was salted quite agreeably. The Rok may have been a disgusting, savage, and ignorant people, but they preserved food well.

"I'll never be the man I was three days ago," Varus said flatly, finally taking more than a few seconds' glance at his arm.

Aristo was surprised by the break in the silence. He was unsure how to respond, or even if he should. They had not spoken of the ramifications of the Rok's torture since leaving the camp. "No one will question your honor or loyalty to the Republic. You have given more service than many Legionaries have within the whole of their term." Anything was a better response than silence, he decided. He knew he had to do something to help preserve Varus' good morale. He had seen so many soldiers accept defeat in their hearts, and that acceptance quickly turned into actual defeat on the battlefield.

"I am not ashamed of what they did to me," Varus stated. "But it means I cannot continue to serve in the Legion. As I always have."

"I would not be so sure of that, Brother," Aristo reassured, the small smile returning. "You have skill in your one hand that many men do not have in two. You know of Graxeis. He had one hand

and one eye, and was champion of the Republic arena for nearly six years, undefeated when he stepped down. You can still fight."

"I am a strong fighter, yes. But I am not Graxeis."

"I would still rather have you at my side than any two Praetorians with whom I've served," Aristo said. He debated with himself if he should call attention to the wound. "At least it was only your shield hand. You are a far cry from a legless cripple who sharpens blades and polishes armor all day. You are far from your prime." He hoped this tactic would help to ease his comrade's mind.

"I would like to believe I have a future use, even if I no longer have a place on the battlefield."

"I would not be so swift in your conclusions," Aristo stated as he rose to his feet. Varus quickly followed suit. The Praetorians stood atop the hill and scanned the area of their retreat. At first, Aristo tried clinging to the hope that his capture had made him overly cautious. But the sound of breaking branches and hoof beats upon the frozen earth was unmistakable. The Rok had found them.

"I had hoped we'd have more time," Varus grunted.

"So had I." Aristo glanced about at their supplies; two Praetorian shields, two Gladius, and two Rok spears were all they had with which to defend themselves. It was a vastly uninspired arsenal, but they would use the weapons to full measure.

"It sounds like cavalry. We face them here?" Varus asked. They shared an uneasy glance as they prepared themselves for what was coming.

"Yes, here. The hill will slow their mounts, and the rocks may protect us from being overrun for a time. Fleeing to open ground is a sure death. It is here, and here only."

So they armed themselves. Aristo helped strap Varus' left arm firmly into his shield. The man grunted as Aristo pulled the leather buckles taught. "Is that too much?" Aristo asked.

"It is not a pleasant feeling. I would rather my arm hurt and my shield stay attached." The men each withdrew their Gladius and tucked it into the small cradle on the inside face of their shields. The Praetorians crafted their shields for the wielder to fight with a spear or javelin, using the Gladius as a hidden weapon which took little time or maneuverability to have at hand.

Aristo passed one of the Rok spears to his comrade, who held it point down with the intention of throwing the weapon. Aristo grasped the other spear and felt the weight and balance of it. The Rok spears were larger than the Praetorian style and meant for melee combat instead. But Varus was confident in his choice of tactics, being one of the finest javeliniers in the Century.

"When they come, we shall take position here." Aristo pointed at the largest of the rocks atop the hill. It was not even knee-high, but it would at least present the most formidable obstacle to charging horses. "You will put the rock to your shield side, and I will take your sword side."

"With any luck, the barbarians are too dumb to surround us," Varus said with a hint of sarcasm.

"With any luck."

Movement ahead was obscured by the tree branches at the bottom of the hill. They could feel the Rok closing in on them like a physical, pressing force. The Barbarians broke the thick tree line at the base of the hill; five behemoths clad in leather and fur, mounted on monstrously huge steeds, emerged from the wood. The barbarians shouted in their guttural gibberish while they glared at the Praetorians standing defiantly atop the hill crest.

"I loathe that thing they call a language," Aristo said.

"Either way, we won't have to listen to their dog's barking much longer," Varus replied. They shared a morbid chuckle.

The Rok had few skills, obnoxious volume being one of them. No further cavalry exited the tree line, so it would be five mounted against two on foot. On flat terrain, that would have been nearly insurmountable odds for infantry, but the steep hill might be enough to offer a chance at survival. The Rok were armed with axes and bludgeons, and very lightly armored, they sported only a single helmet amongst the five. They had no bows or spears with them, so all the Legionaries could do was wait.

"I have had enough of their squawking," Aristo said through clenched teeth. "Praetorian!" he shouted with all the might he could muster.

"Praetorian!" Varus echoed. They chanted the word in unison, the battle cry of a two-man army.

The largest of the riders heeled his horse on at the noise, heading the charge as the remaining four followed suit. The grade of the hill certainly slowed the gargantuan steeds, but the horses galloped forcefully up the steep incline despite the uneven ground, mostly unhindered. Aristo tightly gripped the Rok spear.

He could now see the individual features of each of the five riders. It surprised him when he felt Varus take a half step to his front. His comrade raised the Rok spear and took aim for the briefest of moments before sending the shaft flying through the air. The spear struck the lead rider in the left eye with enough force to whip his head back. Aristo could have sworn he heard the bones in the man's neck snap like splintered wood. The enormous bulk of the rider toppled from the back of his mount and fell to the ground, smashing his head against the frozen earth. With a single throw of his spear Varus had slain his target three times over.

Varus quickly returned to formation and gave Aristo a look as if to say, "Your turn."

Aristo changed the grip on his spear and lifted it to shoulder height. Like many Rok things, the spear was of poor construction, the weight much greater than that to which he was accustomed. The balance was not well-centered at all. Aristo took aim at the closest barbarian rider and let the spear loose. The throw was not the Praetorian's finest. Aristo grimaced as the tip of the spear pitched low, missing the rider completely but burying itself into the long neck of the Rok's horse. The steed screamed and crumbled to the ground. The two riders behind the horse collided with the fallen body, and the three barbarians came down in a jumbled heap.

There was a moment of relief as the five charging mounts had suddenly been reduced to a single rider. The last mounted Rok screamed as he made ready to slam into the Legionaries. Aristo and Varus had their Gladius drawn from the cradle in their shields and at the ready. In tandem, the two Praetorians stepped to their sword side just before the Barbarian rammed into the shield wall. Even as a glancing blow, the force of the rider was mammoth. It took all that Aristo and Varus had left to keep their feet. They pressed the flat of their shields against the enormous horse that was right on them while defending the blows of its rider with their blades.

The two Legionaries were able to get the right leverage they needed and used the rock against which they'd positioned themselves to stagger and overturn the horse and its rider. The barbarian fell from his seat, dragging his mount down with him. The Rok lay at the feet of the two Praetorians, and their Gladius struck quickly, piecing the man's breast twice each. The massive barbarian cried out as blood quickly seeped from the wounds on his chest, killing him.

Aristo and Varus turned to face the Rok who had risen from the collision moments ago. It was now two on foot against three on foot. These were very favorable odds for the Praetorians. One of the three Rok recklessly charged the two Praetorians' shields. Varus body-checked the barbarian with his shield as the man savagely reigned down blow after blow with the two wooden clubs he held in his hands. Aristo maneuvered to the Rok's flank and deftly snaked his arm around the corner of his shield to slip his Gladius between the ribs of the Rok attacker. He sank his blade deep, piercing a lung and the man's heart. The Rok fell without a sound. It was now two on foot against two on foot.

The two reaming barbarians pressed in on the Legionaries. One of the Rok swung a gigantic two-handed axe with immeasurable force and firmly embedded the blade in Varus's shield amid an explosion of wooden splinters. Varus was unable to keep his shield at the ready with his crippled left side against the bulging arms of the axe-wielding Rok. His attacker jerked on the haft of his axe and forced Varus to his knees. Aristo rushed the axeman with his shield, keeping the final Rok at bay with the point of his Gladius. Varus came up with a strike which drove the tip of his Gladius into the Rok's groin, severing the artery in his leg.

It was two against one now. The final Rok lunged at Aristo with a jagged hand axe. Aristo did not have an angle to thrust with his Gladius, so instead he swung it at the Rok's head. The Gladius was primarily a piecing weapon, but Aristo's arm was strong enough to strike a blow with the edge of the blade that cracked open the final Rok's skull.

And then the victors looked over the bodies of the fallen for signs of life. There were none. The Praetorians stood tall and inhaled heavy breath after heavy breath of the icy air.

It was not long after the combat ended that more Rok emerged from the wood. There were many more than five, close to thirty by the time they gathered.

"We cannot fight so many," Aristo said grimly.

"No. We cannot," Varus answered.

"Even on foot they will overtake us."

"They will not overtake you," Varus stated with certainty. Aristo stared at his comrade, unable to find his voice and hoping he would not have to. "You will retreat," Varus continued, "and I will hold them here."

"We will fight them together!" Aristo would argue this until the Rok weapons fell upon them.

"Then we will die together," Varus said, but it was not in confidence. He could not sit with the folly of it. "Only one of us needs to perish here. You should go, and then one of us might live."

Aristo battled with the reality. If they both fought, or both tried to flee, the Rok would eventually overwhelm them. Varus spoke an unarguable truth, but Aristo could not come to grips with abandoning his comrade. Not now. "Why should it be you who dies today?" he said. "If it is about your hand, you have proven that the loss of it makes you no less a warrior."

"It is not about my hand. It is a simple thing. You are a father. I am not. Even though you may be willing to die here, I will see no more half-orphaned Praetorian children," Varus said firmly. Aristo was speechless again. There would be no reasoning with the man. "I will make sure that you have plenty of time," Varus continued. "By the time I surrender this hill, the Rok will care nothing for the one who escaped. They will only wish to finish me." His voice was filled with unshakable resolve.

"What can I do?" Aristo asked. He could do one last thing for his fellow. "Name it, and I will see it done."

"My wife, Persephine. See that she is cared for." Varus choked briefly on her name, but his eyes were clear and he held his head high.

"It is done."

"Go, Brother," Varus said, hurriedly glancing at the oncoming Rok. "There is no more time." They shared a fast, hard embrace.

"You deserved better. It is my honor," Aristo said.

"We all deserved better. It is my honor as well," Varus replied.

Aristo withdrew as fast as his legs would carry him. He felt the pain in his spirit more profoundly than that of the countless wounds of his flesh or the burning of the icy air in his straining lungs. Here he was, fleeing from battle, while a magnificent soldier, a Praetorian, a brother, fought so he could live. The defeat in it, the helplessness, was the greatest shame Aristo had ever known. He would live while a better man died.

For Aristo, today would be that day.

...and I, possessed of patience without boundary, will see that, unless flame of life is tended ever vigilantly, darkness will consume the light...

—Excerpt from the Personal Writings of the Fourth Horseman

Born of Titians

Part 3

Night in the Republic Capital was always noisy. After the tasks of the day had been completed, the citizens of the Republic hurriedly busied themselves with play and recreation. The markets turned from row after row of merchant booths, where trinkets and trifles were peddled, to kiosks, where wine and sweet meats were served in excess. The grand arena may have fallen silent if any games had taken place that day, but every night, the underground spawned to life, offering the spectacle of the pit where men could lay coin on all manner of blood-sport. Doors to the flesh houses were opened for those with carnal needs as pressing as they were exotic.

The Praetorians were a polar people. In the light of the day, they were marvelously disciplined soldiers, eloquent statesmen, and learned scholars. But by night, they became a Republic of vice-driven gluttons. The noises of bargaining, debates, and authoritative commands piercing the air turned to the music of the baser self, a howling cacophony of pleasure and pain.

Aristo found himself subject to noise of a different sort. While the tavern in which he drank was filled with the boisterous commotion of men in drink and games of chance, the rehearsed flirtations of the prostitutes in the front, and practiced moans of the whores in the back, the Legionary's ears were deaf to them. Aristo heard not the sounds of the world around him, but the cries of his own inner torment.

Since his return to the Republic Capital, he had been plagued by the screams of a guilty conscience. The days following his escape had gone so swiftly by, without time to properly process what they really meant. Now, in the relative stillness and safety of the Capital, the Legionary had found himself with ample time to reflect on his choices, struck with the consequences of what he had done—or rather, what he had allowed to happen. Above all, his choice to abandon a wounded brother-in-arms and leave him to a second capture, further torture, mutilation, and most assuredly death. Aristo knew in his head that staying to fight the Rok alongside Varus would have only meant the same fate for himself, but his sense of honor and loyalty objected loudly to the prudence of retreat. Even knowing that Varus was at peace with the decision could not assuage the shameful thoughts clouding his mind. Death before Cowardice. It was the Praetorian way, but it was not the choice Aristo had made.

In the short months during which Aristo had recuperated from his capture and torture, his body had mended with impressive speed under the care of the Legion's Medicus. But his spirit had fallen in equal proportions. The only solace the man could find at first had been at the bottom of a cup. Now, Aristo required the bottom of a jug should he hope to find a moment's peace. He had known the taste of wine before, though he never indulged to excess but on rare occasions. The credit had fallen to his discipline as a soldier and the well-intentioned objections of his wife, though now Aristo questioned his worth as a soldier, and the screaming of his wife was drowned out by the screaming of his conscience.

Aristo craved the setting of the sun. It meant that he was free to pursue some small comfort, away from the judgmental glares of his wife and son, until the breaking of dawn the following day. He had slept only a few nights since his return, and those had been in initial recovery under the wary care of the Medicus. He had turned to drinking himself into blackness for some fleeting hours. Tonight, he hoped his ritual might continue undisturbed. He was well on his way to full inebriation and, with any fortune, would soon be unconscious.

He raised the cup to his lips only to find it dry, then went to pour himself another from the jug sitting at his table. It, too, was exhausted. Aristo allowed himself the briefest moment of displeasure before he waived to one of the servers and ordered another bottle of wholly inexpensive swill. He received it like a man greets rain after a long summer's drought and drank deeply from the eagerly awaited cup.

Sometimes, he found himself replaying Varus' sacrifice and all which had happened that day. Other times, the visions he called were of what might have happened had he stayed alongside his brother, or had he been the one to stay behind. In response, his mind presented him with cruel fantasies of what life might have been like were Varus to have survived the battle in the Rok lands. Perhaps the most vicious daydreams conjured were scenes of Varus' body parts hung from the rancid hide sashes of the barbarians. They had taken his fingers and surely would not have stopped there. Nearly thirty Rok had caught up with them that day, and each savage would have wanted a trophy to mark the defeat of the man who had put them to such a task.

Why him? Why had it been Aristo to live that day, and not Varus? The Legionary asked himself that question more times than he could count but was never satisfied with the answer. In the end, it had been the mere strength of Varus' will which had determined everything. Aristo would have thought that that fact alone would be enough to silence his guilt, but understanding a choice and accepting it were two different things. He could not accept that Varus' choice to die had been solely because Aristo was a father. Even were it true, that Varus' lack of progeny had consigned the man to sacrifice himself, it could hardly have been purely genuine. Was fatherhood really a thing to make one man's life so much greater in value than another's?

Aristo had sworn to look after Varus' wife and had kept his word to a point. But making good and keeping good on that promise had been a greater challenge than he had expected. He had only seen Varus' wife once since returning to the Republic Capital, the day he had told her that her husband died in service to the Legion and had saved Aristo's life. He had felt the blame of a shattered woman scathing him from behind her tearful eyes and could not bear the sight of her after that day. He saw to it that she was finically provided for, but that was the extent of what he could bring himself to do, and the crux of his disgrace.

He drained the last few drops of wine from his cup and promptly upended the jug for the last of it. His hands shook, slipped as he poured, and spilled more than an acceptable amount on the table. This was what the Legionary worked so hard to find, night after night. And soon, very soon, the deathlike sleep which only strong drink could bring would find him.

The tavern he frequented was not far from his home, but after consuming two jugs of wine, the trip was far from a simple journey. On the outside, Aristo was of fine enough constitution to hold his drink well enough to walk, even past the point which left other men in a drunken stupor. But nighttime in the streets of the Capital was cause for caution in those who traveled. The streets were a twisting and entangled labyrinth of back alleys, hidden alcoves, and obscured thruways. Many men found themselves turned about, their sense of direction incapacitated once the Capital took on its nocturnal guise. Besides those who peddled drink or flesh, there were those who preyed upon the hapless travelers of the night. Thievery was common on the darkened streets of the Capital, and for the gravely unfortunate, so was murder. Aristo made certain to don his purple Legionary's cloak whenever he intended to drink himself into incapacity. The uniform of a professional soldier was often enough to deter any predatory urges lurking in the darkness.

He could feel it now. His belly churned with the drink and his head felt heavy. His time for slumbering oblivion was fast approaching, and with unsteady legs the Legionary stood and left some coin upon the table he had claimed for the last several hours. He was stopped twice on his way out by the prostitutes who worked there, but he turned the women away as he always did. A whore's charm had never managed to cut through what little morals he thought he had left, even when he had been long at drink.

Leaving the shouts and screams of the tavern behind him, he stepped through the doors, into the street, and finally felt a moment's peace. The world around was suddenly much less suffocating, as was the burden of guilt weighing upon his spirit and dominating his mind. A dark and quiet walk back to his home before slipping into nothingness sounded like paradise. The Legionary had managed to put another miserable day behind him, and he would enjoy what time he had left before sleep took him and he awoke to repeat the battle of silencing his conscience.

The streets were well-walked, but the paths underfoot were still largely uneven in places, making him stagger. He stayed close to the building walls lining the street, placing a hand to steady himself each time he felt the drink rob him of his footing. He was almost halfway home when it dawned on him that he could no longer transport the two jugs of wine sloshing in his belly. A stabbing cramp flared in his lower stomach. It struck the man as strange, that one's bladder could suddenly and without warning be a source of such massive discomfort.

The Legionary gave a quick glance about to make sure his back would not be to any hopeful thieves, but he saw the small street populated only by the slumbering, malnourished forms of a few homeless beggars. He placed one hand on a wall and used the other to loosen his garments. He sighed in relief as his bladder emptied onto the building's rough stone.

Finished, Aristo stepped from the darkened side street and was suddenly overcome with a shooting pain between his shoulder blades. He had never suffered pain without injury and could not place what had caused such a burst of agony. Reaching behind his own shoulder to inspect the surprise, wondering what could possibly make him feel this way, he brought his fingers back up to his face and was shocked to see them covered in blood. His own blood.

Then, as if the sight of his red-stained hands had been a cue, he began a fit of violent coughing. He was then aware of the taste of blood in his mouth, on his lips, and his breath was far too hard to catch as he fell to his knees. He could feel the life flowing from his body. In an instant, he had felt the warmth of alcohol in his belly turn to frost in his blood. It was cold like he had never known—cold beyond cold.

Aristo had no strength left and fell to the dust beneath him. He gazed up to see a figure standing over him as his life ran short. His sight soon faded, but it was still keen enough to see the figure's face. Three images confronted him in his final moments. He had seen war in all its most gruesome atrocities, but the tear-stained face of this demure little woman was the most chilling sight of them all. He saw the knife in her hands soaked to the hilt with his blood; it was Varus' wife Persephine. The last thing Aristo saw in the moments before his sight turned to blackness was the belly of his closest brother's widow round and full with child, and his shame multiplied by a measure beyond counting.

There, in the darkened streets of the Republic Capital, amidst the sand and blood, the Reaper came to collect the Praetorian. Aristo would soon command a Legion of Death, and with it he would bring war and the spectacle of slaughter.

...On the day of the Shattering, the first and only tears to pass from the eyes of Death were wept. They fell from Paradise to the realm of man, bringing with them sorrow, grief, and mourning. And some of Death's tears fell further. They descended to land far beyond the light and warmth of Paradise. They struck barren ground, where there was no life, only darkness and cold—cold beyond cold. And from these tears of anguish, pain, torment, suffering, fear, and despair sprang forth a great and flowing river. The river would come to claim the spirits of those who stood guilty and condemned when they departed the realm of man. The river's name was Praytos, and Death built his kingdom of Purgatory upon its shores...

—Excerpt from the Book of Life

The Kiss

Part 1

They told her she was not beautiful, and those words were as cruel as they were false. Her beauty would become a thing of legend and myth, only to be matched by her tragedy. Her scarlet lips would end the lives of countless men.

Lady Kathryn Petra was to become a woman soon. That was the day of which most young girls of the nobility dreamed. It was the day she would receive her first suitors.

Kathryn was the youngest of Lord Petra's three daughters, though sadly she was also said to be the plainest. The eldest of the Lord's girls, Katlin, was a striking woman, and her beauty was held in the highest esteem. The middle daughter Kailin was not as fair as her elder sister, but the woman had developed many talents. Lady Kailin could play half a dozen instruments, had a magnificent soprano voice, and could wield a writer's quill or artist's brush as well as most seasoned practitioners of the craft. Sadly, among all the courts of the aristocracy, Lady Kathryn Petra was unanimously said to be the lesser of the Lord's three children.

For all the rumor-mongering and gossip around the qualities of Lord Petra's progeny, Lady Kathryn did not care for nor place any high value on the words of sycophants and trained liars. She nurtured no jealousy toward the sisters whom others thought to be so vastly superior. Kathryn loved her sisters dearly, was inspired by their beauty and talents where others coveted and envied them.

Lord Petra's youngest daughter was filled with hope and joy today. She knew her father had arranged for nearly all the finest young men the nobility had to offer to call upon her. But Kathryn was only concerned with the attention of one man.

His name was Alexi, and he was the youngest son of Lord Markov. Alexi's father ruled the province on Lord Petra's northern border. The families were geographically close, but a tighter bond had been formed when both Lord Petra and Lord Markov commissioned as Commandants together for the whole of the Ten Year Winter Siege. The Lords were true brothers-in-arms, and as such, their children had grown up together.

Kathryn had long been smitten with Alexi. It had started one summer as a sense of admiration for the boy. In the warmer months, a thaw arrived in the Grey Mountains of Lord Markov's province; the melting ice brought a host of dangers, making travel in the Grey Mountains a dangerous and sometimes fatal proposition. As a cautious man, Markov called upon Petra's hospitality in the summer months, which would host Markov's two sons until the first freezing of the year.

While residing at Petra's court, Alexi and Androv were treated as family. That meant that the brothers received the schooling and attention of Lord Petra's private tutors, who also taught his own daughters.

Kathryn had met Alexi for the first time when she was only five years old. She'd had some difficulty in her father's stables during a riding lesson. Her white stallion Kita was freshly broken yet still tended to shy from the feel of a saddle. Kathryn was intimidated by the giant beast, but Alexi had been so brave. Despite only being eight years old himself, Alexi had helped saddle Kita and calmly led the stallion around the riding track not once, but twice. The boy was a living tribute to the Markov creed. "No fear. No death." Kathryn had followed the boy with a youthful, wide-eyed sparkle at every opportunity following that first morning.

Soon, summer was the only time that existed for Kathryn, the remainder of the year a fragmented blur of images and sounds. Kathryn longed for those few and fleeting months when Alexi would return to court. The children had grown close over the years, and she was so deeply relieved to discover that her feelings were not unrequited. They shared knowing smiles and countless hours of laughter as the world turned around them. Alexi made Kathryn's world so much more bearable in spite of those who only saw the plain and youngest daughter of her father. He never failed to make her feel radiant and beautiful.

Now, Lady Kathryn waited with baited breath in her father's great hall for the first of her suitors. She anxiously wondered how many boys she would have to see before she had the opportunity to be with Alexi, to laugh with him about the whole thing. The hall was colder than usual, with no one left to tend the fires once the servants had been cleared out. Custom bade courtship to be a private matter, and one of the few times in a Lord or Lady's life where they would not be constantly stifled by attendants. With the fire slowly dying, Kathryn felt the cold nip at her fingertips as she watched her breath turn into thin frost in the air.

The creaking of the hinges on the thick pine doors filled the hall as they opened. She felt the rush of blood as her heart beat faster, hoping the herald would announce Alexi.

"His Lord Vladof's eldest son, Mordechai," came the distant call of the herald from beyond the doors. Lady Kathryn felt her heart sink a little in her breast, a stab of disappointment.

She rose to her feet as Mordechai entered the hall, the sound of his footsteps booming off the walls as the thick heels of his jackboots struck the stones underneath. The boy bowed once he reached Kathryn and waited for her to acknowledge him with a curtsy. After the obligatory introductions and other required matters of state, they were able to sit back and speak freely. The conversation was neither dull nor unpleasant, and Lord Mordechai was very curios and polite, but Lady Kathryn could not help it that her thoughts continually drifted to Alexi.

Then Lord Mordechai properly excused himself when it was time for the next suitor. Sadly, the following man she received was not Alexi, nor the suitor after him, nor even the suitor after him. Lady Kathryn felt her heart would turn as cold as the dwindling fireplace the longer she went without seeing the one and only man she ever wanted on that day. Finally, after a lengthy string of undesirables and the accompanying forced pleasantries of etiquette, the herald announced Lord Alexi Markov.

Kathryn's eyes shown like the dawn when she first saw him, her darling Alexi. He had grown so much since the previous summer. His shoulders were broad like his father's, and his beautiful blond hair now almost reached his perfectly squared jaw. She met his striking blue gaze as he bowed to her, and she nearly fell to the cold stone floor.

"My warmest greetings to you on this cold day, Lady Kathryn Petra," Alexi said in a newfound voice which commanded the power of the ocean yet was gentle as a flowing mountain brook.

"And my warmest greetings to you on this cold day, Lord Alexi Markov." She had to summon all the will she could to pass the words without error. Despite her proper execution of the expected greeting, she felt her cheeks flushing hot and wondered just how embarrassingly red they had become.

There was a brief moment of silence as they took in the sight of each other, for the first time as man and woman. Alexi's attentive eyes quickly took stock of the sparsely decorated room, noted the chill on Kathryn's breath. "I see your fire has nearly died. It's quite cold today. Would you allow me to tend to the flames?" he asked softly.

"Yes, I would like that. You are kind to think of my comfort." It always amazed her that Alexi never failed to note her comfort, that he still made every effort to foster her happiness.

Alexi deftly rekindled the smoldering embers wasting away in the fire place. They sat and enjoyed the fresh rush of heat as it quickly washed through the hall. "I hope your journey from the Grey Mountains was swift and without incident," Kathryn said. It seemed so hard now to start simple conversation with him. She was not as skilled as her sister Kailin in the art of small talk, but she could hold intelligent discourse. Fortunately, she never had to stress for words when it came to Alexi.

"Yes, our travel was uneventful, and I would like to extend my sincerest gratitude for your Lord father's hospitality on behalf of the family Markov," Alexi said with poise. The young Lord paused briefly as he considered his next words. "I must confess I was looking forward to seeing you again. I always enjoy our moments together."

Kathryn felt as though her heart had grown wings, and she subtly clutched her chest for fear it might take flight. "Your words are most kind, Alexi. I fear I must make the same confession." She failed completely in hiding the broad smile on her vermilion-painted lips. But she didn't need to hide it when Alexi smiled back.

They sat at great length in the hall, candidly speaking of this and that, fond memories, hopes, and fears. Of all the people in the world, Alexi was the only one with whom she could simply be Kathryn, and not Lady Kathryn Petra, youngest of her father's children. And then the moment came when Kathryn noticed some foreboding sadness take ahold of him, a nameless thing, solemn and sad, reflecting in his deep blue eyes. The joy and laughter faded from the room into a deathly silence. "Does something trouble you, My Lord?" she asked, hoping she had simply misread his expression.

Alexi fought to phrase his next words. She watched the young Lord struggle with what he wanted to say. "Kathryn, we both know what is to happen today," he finally said.

"Yes. I am being courted and soon will be betrothed." The words felt foolish on her lips but she said them with a smile, hiding the anxiety of what was to come next.

Again, Alexi fought with what he wanted to say, and after several unbearable moments of silence, he spoke. "I do not mean to presume, but I feel we both understand this one thing. Of all the men you have seen today, you only have eyes for me." It nearly broke him to speak the words.

Once more, silence filled the room, and the young Lady Petra had to beat back a well of tears before she responded. "Alexi, you are the only man I have ever desired. I have long wished to be yours, and only yours."

"I know. I have felt this for some time now." He took a deep breath and steadied his shaking hands. "Kathryn, I love you. I love you deeply, and I have loved you for so many years." He used every ounce of resolve at his disposal to force his voice to obey. He watched Kathryn's face light like the sun on a cloudless day atop the summit of the Grey Mountains.

"Alexi..." she stammered.

"But..." he interjected, stopping her before she could speak at any length. "Even for all my love for you, I cannot be your suitor. I can never ask for your hand." His courage seemed to last only as long as the words he spoke with surprising speed.

As high as Kathryn's heart had just soared, it sank now with equally terrifying speed. "I don't understand. Please tell me why." She blinked, and a trail of tears left its mark upon her face.

"I feel something within the core of my bones," he said, "and I realized it has been in me all my life." Kathryn hung on his every word. "I feel the call to serve in the priesthood of the White Lady Winter. It means I must never marry." He took a deep breath and sighed, but his brow furrowed in concern for his dearest friend.

"I admire your devotion," Kathryn managed, the tears running freely now. "But you can piously serve the White Lady as a Lord just as well as you might in the priesthood."

Alexi looked long at the woman he loved, studied the pain in her eyes, and searched for truth in his words as his eyes, too, filled with tears. "I can't," he whispered. "Kathryn, I'm sorry to have hurt you. It was never what I wanted." He gently took her hands and searched her face for some glimmer of understanding.

But there was none. "I don't understand," Kathryn repeated over and over through her tears, her hands limp in his. Alexi tried to console her, but to no avail. It was as though she no longer registered his presence. When there were no more words to be spoken, Alexi left Lord Petra's hall, and they parted ways.

Kathryn saw no more suitors after Alexi. She sat alone for hours in her father's great hall with only the ashes of a long-extinguished fire to keep her company. Then she sent word to her father that she would take any suitor who would have her; she cared not who he was.

She felt as though the chill in the air had turned her heart to a block of ice. The girl who had once been so full of joy and life had died, and now only bitterness and a lust for the unattainable animated her flesh. Lady Kathryn Petra felt the change come over her. Today, she had indeed become a woman, had felt her first great loss as an adult. Alexi's rejection had bewildered her at first but now was only maddening. Two people who loved one another should be together, she told herself. It became a mantra of sorts, that they loved each other, that they should be together. No matter what. Kathryn swore she would do whatever it took to win her Alexi. He would want her, he would crave her, he would desire her. He would lust for her.

She would make him.
For Lady Kathryn Petra, today would be that day.

Abandon all hope, ye who enter here. Within, there is only weeping and the gnashing of teeth.

—Inscription above the Gates of Purgatory

The Kiss

Part 2

And she possessed a tragic beauty, like the stripped branches of a cemetery tree cast against the steel grey sky of autumn. Lady Kathryn Petra had grown into a woman, a magnificent woman. She was no longer the shy and awkward girl, unnoticed by those at court. She had transformed into some otherworldly creature. Still not the physically radiant specimen that her eldest sister was, Kathryn's features were dark, alluring, and seductive. She often let her long black hair fall in her face, flowing about her to obscure those features. She knew that sort of thing made her air of mystery all the more enticing. Her eyes held within them two perfect storms of fury, of lust, and desire. Her skin was deathly pale; even among the fair-skinned people of the Grey Mountains, her flesh stood out. Her lips were a deep, crimson red which contrasted the striking white skin around them. Lady Kathryn Petra—the Kiss of Death, they called her.

Her moniker was well-earned. She had now survived her fifth husband in as many years. Men were drawn to Lady Kathryn and then to their demise. Like a siren, she summoned them to her and enthralled them with her wiles. She had learned that a man's intellect could be swayed by his heart, and the disposition of his heart could be manipulated by the impulses of his loins. She was no harlot, though some would call her such. But only in hushed whispers behind her back. Lady Kathryn traded largely on the promise, rather than the carnal act itself, when dealing with those who pursued her. She had learned to pull the puppet strings attached to a man's baser creature and delighted in seeing men bend to her will. She had grown to love control, the knowledge that, with a stroke of his ego and the batting of her eyes, she could call a man to heel like a trained animal.

Any man, that was, save the one and only she desired. Alexi. How she still yearned for that beautiful, beautiful man. The man who would not have her.

Lady Kathryn derived no real pleasure from influencing her playthings. She was not cruel to the men who lusted after her, not intentionally. Her actions may have been cruel when they suited her purpose, but her heart was calculated and cold. She had felt some measure of pity for the first two husbands, once it came time for them to go. Sergey and Yuri had each been kind enough to her; they never struck her, were gentle and attentive when her role demanded a performance of wifely duties. She had whispered the same stories to them both in the dark hours of the night. It was easy to make them feel invincible, or slighted by Lord So-and-So for some manufactured offence.

It was odd that Lady Kathryn had never set foot on a single battlefield yet had started more wars than any Lord, living or dead. She used her husbands to gain power and military force. It occurred to her long ago that she would need the command of a great host of men were she to accomplish what she'd set out to do. Toppling the priesthood of the White Lady Winter would be no small feat; the supporters of theocracy were both numerous and powerful. Kathryn could not stand the institution which had stolen her Alexi from her—her one, true desire. She would see the followers of that white-faced witch scattered to the wind, her churches in ruin, and then she would have the life with her Alexi which had been denied them.

Not one of the mountain Lords dared think to launch such a brazen attack on the church of the White Lady Winter; that institution could out-spend and out-man any domestic adversary. This was to say nothing of the devout and pious Lords who would pledge their own men to the defense of The White Lady Winter were she openly attacked. No, no one could do it. It was impossible. And Kathryn's first husband Sergey had only a modest fighting force upon which to call. Any uprising would be over faster than the freezing of the fjords in the deep winter.

The notion of overthrowing the White Lady had seemed a child's fantasy until Sergey had the misfortune of insulting Lord Checkov's Maestro during a spring gala. It was a simple exhibition of swordsmanship, and Lord Checkov's finest fencer was also his Maestro. Sergey had been repeatedly humiliated by the other man's prowess and skill, failing to score even a single touch with the blunted sword. Kathryn, ever the opportunist, had taken each of her husband's defeats as an opportunity to spin a web around the men. With each touch, she planted in Sergey's mind the notion that he was up to the challenge of besting Lord Checkov's Maestro. Once she had thoroughly entwined her husband's pride, she was bold enough to quietly infer that the other man had perhaps been cheating.

Sergey had a burning need to maintain his reputation and honor, so he claimed that trial combat and real fighting were two very different things, and that the Maestro would likely not be so fortunate with a real blade. Naturally, Lord Checkov summoned war-ready rapiers at once so they might put to rest such doubt and disrespect. Sergey refused to apologize. Whether it was pride or wine that spoke, no one would ever know. But the duel between Sergey and Lord Checkov's Maestro was over in four phrases, with Sergey's heart run through, leaving him dead on the floor.

Suddenly, Lady Kathryn was a widow and, with no male heir apparent, she was now in command of her late husband's assets. That was when it dawned on her that the means to amass a sizable contending force was, in fact, within her grasp. One dead husband had made her a powerful woman indeed. The resources of several more would give her the army she needed.

At the Czar's winter court that same year, Lady Kathryn caught the eye of her second husband, Yuri. There was an almost forbidden and certainly taboo element about courting a woman who had lost a husband. Several of the mountain Lords found such an illicit thing highly desirable, and Yuri was one of them. Lady Kathryn had stood out so finely that season, still fully clad in the black of grieving. It was simple for her to draw Yuri into her clutches.

She presented herself as vulnerable and damaged when he first introduced himself, and Kathryn convinced the man he was a beacon of might and strength as they walked the dimmed halls of the Czar's palace. She spouted a fountain of sorrow into Yuri's ears, telling him how deeply wounded she had been by the sudden and tragic death of her late husband. Then, she showered him with complements. "Your presence gives me comfort. You are the first man to truly listen to how much pain I feel. Your steady resolve is an inspiration to me." Lady Kathryn listened to him speak at length of himself into the far hours of the night, convincingly seeming to hang on his every word. From that very first night, she knew she had him.

The seduction of Lord Yuri did not take long at all. She

garnered a proposal before winter's end. Others were overtly critical when the engagement was announced, but not so openly vocal about their disapproval. With the joining of their land and forces, Lord Yuri and Lady Kathryn now boasted the sixth largest fighting force in the Grey Mountain range and, more importantly, controlled two thirds of the border between the Gray Mountains and the lowland valleys. This gave the couple powerful sway over any import, export, travel, and trade occurring within the Czar's domain.

But Kathryn was still far from her goal and she knew it. It was not hard to convince her husband that a mere two thirds of the boarders would not suit them, not when they alone could control every pelt of fur or load of coal entering or exiting the Grey Mountains. The idea sold itself; Lady Kathryn barely had to speak it, sealing the plot with the caress of her soft, crimson lips, and the man was prepared for war.

Lord Karston Nikita was the only obstacle between Lord Yuri Magnus and his economic monopoly of the trade roads to the north. Lady Kathryn convinced her husband that Lord Karston was an easy adversary to overcome, though that couldn't have been further from the truth. Lord Karston had a militia as large as Yuri's and was well-loved by the Lords governing the territories to the north and south of his borders. It would, of course, be three against one, with Yuri at the disadvantage.

The true difficulty lay in finding a way to separate her husband's demise from the sure defeat of his entire army. It would not profit her plans against the White Lady were her soon-to-be forces destroyed with her husband. So she had to make Yuri see the glory and the promise of leading his men from the front.

Each night for a full month, Lady Kathryn lay beside her husband and begged him to grace her with exploits of his military genius, of how he planned to gain control of the northern border.

And Yuri's own mouth and inflated vanity dug his very grave. In the end, Lord Yuri voiced the idea first, confident that inspiring the men with his presence in the field was a tactic of his own design.

The war went down in the history archives, though it lasted only a single battle. Lady Kathryn felt some pity for her second husband when she received news that he had fallen at the hands of Lord Karston and his allies. She delighted not in the sacrifice of pawns. Yet her greatest lament was not the loss of her husband, but the loss of nearly a tenth of his fighting men and their lives at the hands of his ego.

After Yuri, there was little difficulty finding suitors. Lady Kathryn alone held formidable resources, coveted by each and every eligible Lord, and it only complimented her dark and entrancing beauty, matured by time and all the more noticeable to the men around her. The widow of the Grey Mountains fast became a living folktale. Some said there was witchcraft about her, but those factions were equally divided as to the manner of such witchcraft, of whether she was a sinister enchantress or merely a victim. But the rumors swirling about the courts of the Mountain Lords could not dissuade them from pursuing her as yet another one of their possessions. This was a hope Lady Kathryn saw plainly when men looked her and a fantasy she cultivated with masterful precision. While others admired and lauded her sisters, it was she alone for whom men lusted.

The next three men whom Lady Kathryn wed all seemed to blur together. She hardly remembered their faces. Yet she remembered vividly how intricate and involved her seduction of each had been. She had made it a point to discover the most intimate details of their lives, every skeleton buried in their past, before they ever met face to face. She excelled at making them feel alive, but once a man was dead, cold, and in the ground, Lady Kathryn scarcely gave him a second thought.

Now, Lady Kathryn Petra of the Grey Mountains had no more cause for subversive plotting and manipulation. Once her fifth husband had met his end that past summer, she commanded the greatest army the Mountain Lords had ever seen. Five houses, now united under one banner, was an awe-inspiring visage. It was time for her to step out of the shadows to which she was so accustomed and to finally make her intentions known to all. It was the culmination of years of meticulous planning; the cost was heavy, and such a precious prize had required great patience. The promise of a union at last with Alexi was all she'd ever dreamed of, and now it was close enough to grasp.

Lady Kathryn planned to take great delight in the destruction of the White Lady's empire. The Grey Mountains had room enough for only one harsh and brutal mistress, and Lady Kathryn Petra intended to be that one.

It was regrettable that the devout followers of the White Lady Winter would inevitably perish in the destruction to come, but Kathryn consoled herself by allowing her forces to make them one offer; those who feared death could always recant their beliefs and be spared. She swore that the White Lady's days as Alexi's only love were nearing their end. Soon she would be with him, together forever. The thought warmed the ice in Kathryn's chest and flushed her snow-white cheeks with a red, girlish glow.

The sound of mounts approaching from outside her carriage returned the Lady's attention and her wits. She parted the red satin curtains from the carriage windows to see the riders outside—Commandant Sierov and his aid.

The Commandant met his Lady's eyes and bowed to her before speaking. "My Lady, we have routed the forces defending this monastery. We are ready for the assault on the keep itself. Shall we begin?" His words rang out through his coarse black beard.

"Not yet. Wait for my coach. I would like to watch as you burn that refuge of the White Lady to the ground." Lady Kathryn let the curtains fall again before she allowed the smile to cross her lips.

My So Enticing Lord Master Death,

I must first confess this is written purely for the sake of personal gratification. I would seek your aid in a matter close to heart. The sixty-sixth day fast approaches, and all eyes shall look to your great spectacle with grand appetite for the wonders to follow in its wake. It has become known that the dark beauty, the one many men called the Kiss of Death, shall be among those who will take part in your masterpiece. At your command, my court has dispatched our finest Reaper, Eutanos, to collect her presently. Clearly, my court shall favor this one in the event, but the question of securing patronage for a chosen spirit is not the reason for this correspondence. My purpose is one of baser and simpler aim.

I have long watched this one in the realm of man, and she is truly a magnificent wonder. I believe the sorted tales of men which boast of her allure. In fact, her beauty transcended the world of the living and reached through the depths of the Praytos to caress the heart beneath my very breast. I would listen to tales no longer.

With your permission, I would know them for myself before she is bound by the events of the sixty-sixth day. I would taste the bitter sweetness of her crimson lips. I would feel the cool touch of her flawless silken skin pressed to mine. I would smell the fragrance of her hair which flows black as the darkest hour of night. I would take delight in all that she is, if you would be so generous as to allow me the privilege.

Yours in Pleasure,

Lady and Lord Lust

The Kiss

Part 3

It would never happen. After all she had done to make it possible, Alexi still would not have her. Lady Kathryn Petra had raised the greatest army any Czar beneath the Grey Mountains had ever seen. She had united the lands of five Lords beneath the flag of a single name. She had brought the forces of the White Lady Winter to their knees before her. She had made the priesthood change the very foundation of canon law. In the end, it had all been without use.

The man whom Lady Kathryn loved with every measure of her enchanting being remained unmoved from his religious devotion. All these years later, her love for him was still unrequited, and it was more than she could bear. She had done all she could think to do, and yet her efforts were still found wanting. Lady Kathryn could not continue to live in a world where she and Alexi were not as one. She would sooner see every last piece of ice at the summit of the Grey Mountains melt and wash away all which lay in their shadow than be apart from him but a moment longer.

Most of the Lords would give up anything to accomplish what she had or to possess what she possessed. Each one of them spent the whole of their lives chasing elevation and advantage. Lady Kathryn Petra had built a vast empire, feared by all, even the Czar, but it was an empty empire. She had never set out to build herself an unassailable force. The ends had never been about conquest, and her goal was not about usurping control. All Lady Kathryn wanted was Alexi. He alone was the sole reason for every life ended and every keep burned by the orders of Lady Kathryn. No one understood the truth behind her motives.

In the courts of the Lords and Czar, Lady Kathryn Petra was heralded as a brilliant political mind and a master strategist, whose maneuvering and plots stood as an example to be admired and followed. But the reality was that she was simply a zealously impassioned woman driven by a singular lust. Nobody realized that she cared for one purpose and one purpose alone. Her willingness to sacrifice anything in order to be closer to that which she craved was not seen for what it was. Men saw Lady Kathryn as a viscous iron maiden, the Kiss of Death, but the only thing she had ever wanted was the love of her beautiful Alexi.

She recounted the final days before she brought the cursed White Lady's priests under her heel. She had put nearly every abbey, chapel, and monastery in the land to ruin. The army of the White Lady had been broken, all of the Lords who supported the priesthood slain, routed, or swayed to Lady Kathryn's side. Finally, the archbishop of the White Lady had sued for peace. He would give Lady Kathryn anything her heart desired to cease her attack on the priesthood.

He was a frightened little man of advanced years, but his station commanded great authority and power. The archbishop was not like the Lords and Ladies of the nobility, consumed with motives extending no further than their own personal comfort and gratification. He was a genuinely faithful man who believed in the doctrine of the White Lady. The archbishop had never used his power for his own gain and thought only of the good of his fellow believers. In essence, he was a true rarity in the world. He was a good man. There might have once been a time when the manipulation and intimidation of such a man would have given Lady Kathryn pause, but such days were long a thing of memory. She was now far too driven by her own ends that the cost of achieving them meant nothing to her. Everything and everyone was expendable, even a good man.

He had struck Lady Kathryn as meek and pitiful when they first met to discuss the terms of peace. It might as well have been an offer of surrender with the way the archbishop behaved. There was no negotiation on his part whatsoever; he was fully agreeable to any and every one of Lady Kathryn Petra's demands. He offered no resistance and was fully dominated by the woman. She had known the remaining forces of the White Lady were in no position to make demands, but she had at least expected a play at resolve, or at the very least the guise of dignity. She had to mask her surprise with how easily the man crumbled. She was used to men falling to her charms and had used her wiles on more than one member of the priesthood, but still she had expected more from the archbishop.

Lady Kathryn had to conceal her true intention within a slew of other demands. She demanded the priesthood suspend the long winter's rest indefinitely. She required there to be no more than one abbey located within each province. Lady Kathryn wanted all the statues depicting the White Lady Winter removed from any place of public viewing. Her list went on and on. It was a small item, inserted toward the end of her demands, which held all the significance for the task of subjugating the priesthood of the White Lady. She asked that the members of the priesthood be allowed to marry and take a wife in wedlock. The archbishop granted the request without contest, and Lady Kathryn Petra felt the swell of triumph. She would soon be with her darling Alexi.

After that day, she could not wait for the moment when she could next be with him. Within the fortnight, she had learned of his location and made with great speed to meet him. She had not set eyes on Alexi since that day so long ago, when what should have been courtship revealed itself as rejection.

He resided at one of the White Lady's last standing abbeys. It was the largest in the land and also housed a monastery for newly sworn priests to begin their studies and reflections. Lady Kathryn wanted to despise the stone and glass of the place Alexi had called home for so long, but she could not fully quell a measure of awe taking root when she saw the sheer size of the abbey. She had never cared to lay sight on the place until she realized it held her Alexi within its walls. At least the size of the Czar's palace, the abbey sat atop a sharp cliff face, and its south-side vista overlooked a sprawl of snow-covered earth below until the eyes could see no further. Lady Kathryn would never confess it aloud, but this abbey was a thing of beauty. She hated the notion that the cruel White Lady Winter, responsible for claiming Alexi's heart, could command something so regal and serene.

Lady Kathryn's coach brought her to the abbey's courtyard, where she waited to be received. She had to keep the red blinds in the coach drawn over the windows to avoid subjection to the horrid displays of the countless busts, tapestries, and stained-glass etchings of the White Lady Winter. She was not left waiting longer than a few breaths of chilled air, but every moment in this place was beyond her comfort.

The abbot himself called on Lady Kathryn and welcomed her. She dispensed with formal pleasantries, easily detecting the loathing and duress behind the abbot's forced smile. She knew that, unlike the archbishop, were the abbot to have his way he would have seen her pale skin, raven hair, and crimson lips over the side of the cliff. The abbot shared sentiments with most of the remaining White Lady's devoted. They all cursed the name of Petra and the witch of a woman the bloodline had spawned. Lady Kathryn had to imagine it a horrible thing, to have a stranger wrest away the core of one's religion only to leave it an eviscerated husk. That thought, along with the unified anger of the White Lady's followers, warmed Lady Kathryn's icy-fair skin and graced her fine, red lips with a smile.

The abbot brought Lady Kathryn to a large hall. It struck her how similar the hall was to the very one in her childhood home where she had last seen Alexi. The fire even burned low like it had on that day. This time, though, the chill in the air did not bother Lady Kathryn Petra. She dismissed the abbot, an act silently welcomed with delight by both parties, and took a place in front of the fire to wait for her Alexi. She watched the dying embers amid the fireplace, fading from glowing orange to an ashen grey.

The doors to the hall opened like that day long ago, and once again, there stood her darling Alexi. He had matured into even more of a man than she had ever believed possible. It defied all logic and reason how one committed to the modest, humble life of a priest could possess such a resplendent beauty; somehow, Alexi made this possible. He approached her with a gorgeously melancholy expression and stood silently.

Lady Kathryn Petra had spent many hours rehearsing what she would say to Alexi when the day came that they would finally be returned to each other. How desperately she had longed to pass those carefully selected words through her lips, but in those first few moments standing before him, once again, she was lost for all words. She could only drink in the splendor of this man for whom she had moved the very foundation of monarchy and religion. She could not remember how long they stood without speech; she only recalled it was the tearful look in Alexi's eyes as he turned to leave that spurred her to breach that silence.

Lady Kathryn had exploded into a flurry of words when it seemed the continued silence might separate her from him. She spoke with all the joy and hope of the innocent girl she had once been. In an instant, all the poise and refined discipline, the detachment she had honed over the years, vanished. She reaffirmed her love for Alexi. She spoke of how her five husbands never held her heart as he did. She told him of how she had carefully maneuvered the will of so many men so they could be together. She unfolded the story of how she changed the bedrock of religious canon for the sake of her devotion to him. She expressed her elation that now, nothing more stood in the way of their marriage. By the end of her rambling, she was out of breath and close to tears.

The response Alexi gave on that day was anything but that which would fulfill her hopes. Instead, it utterly crushed her spirit. Alexi was so angry he nearly struck her. The priest flew into an animalistic rage, cursing Kathryn for a harlot and a villain. He said she had brought irreparable shame and disgrace upon the honorable name of her father and her house and called her a murderer. He said he felt as though he should cut the beating heart from his very chest for committing the offence of ever feeling love for a monster as vile as Lady Kathryn Petra. He branded her a liar and hypocrite, saying her love for him was false and that she knew nothing of his heart if she would so eagerly see all he ever held dear burned to nothing. She had destroyed his faith, and he hated her for it. Alexi's raving was punctuated by the slamming of wood against stone as he stormed out, shutting the doors to the hall behind him with such force it rattled the glass in the great room's windows.

Lady Kathryn was left in the frigid air of the vast, empty room—beyond grief, beyond sorrow, beyond tears. Like a walking corpse, she wandered in a haze back to her coach. She had little memory of the events after leaving the abbey, could not recall giving the order or witnessing its results. But she knew the abbey had burned by her command, along with all who remained inside, including Alexi. She wanted nothing to remind her of the man who refused to love her. But that was impossible. Everywhere Kathryn looked, she saw Alexi's accusing gaze.

If it was not something to remind her of the love she lost, then it was something to remind her of the dammed White Lady Winter who stole him away. Snow and ice. Everywhere in the mountains there was snow and ice, like the White Lady still mocked Lady Kathryn, carelessly flaunting her charms. Lady Kathryn bore the following days with dwindling resolve. She was haunted and relentlessly tormented by the memories of yet another rejection. And she would endure these memories no longer.

Lady Kathryn now stood in her private chambers, disrobed before a steaming bath. The air in the room sent chills along her skin. Slowly, she entered the giant brass tub and let the warm, soothing water gently wash over her flawless white flesh. The heat relaxed all the muscles in her body, and the discomfort of her own skin to which she had become so accustomed slowly faded away beneath the lapping of the warm water.

This was the most peace she had felt in longer than she could recall. She was ready for what was to come. In fact, she welcomed it. With a few swift motions and a flash of steel, she drew two thin lines of scarlet down her arms. The water, once clear and hot, quickly turned a murky red. And cold—cold beyond cold.

Lady Kathryn Petra felt release as the blood trickled out of her veins. Finally, it would stop. Finally, she could be somewhere with her beautiful Alexi, where there was no White Lady Winter. They would finally be together

Then, under the shadow of night in the silent and darkened room, the Reaper came to collect the Kiss of Death from the crimson waters. And she, possessed of a tragic beauty, would become the object of his desire.

"I watch over this one and I weep for him. His might is unmatched, his spirit truly without the root of fear. Yet he is so deeply enveloped by the clutches of Wrath, it breaks the heart. I scream at him, pleas of mercy and serenity upon the autumn wind, but my words remain unheard. I try in vain to offer comfort to a troubled mind. His spirit craves the spilling of blood, and even for all my efforts there is no end to its thirst. I dread that the depths of the Praytos will take this one."

—Utania, Valkyrie of Peace

Vengeful Ghost

Part 1

It was said he could not be defeated. It was said he had slain over ten thousand warriors. It was said he had lived for nine hundred years and would live for nine hundred more. It was said that his father was the strike of lightning and his mother the winter's frost, that he traded his spirit to a demon for the strength of twenty men. It was said his blades were forged from the teeth of dragons and his armor fashioned from the bones of giants.

No one knew how much was myth and how much truth save for this: he was the Fist of the Shogunate, the finest of warriors and the most brutal of killers. His thirst for blood and glory was unquenchable. His name was Kenji Rei.

In the final days of autumn, the air was filled with the crisp bite of the coming winter. The Emperor's court found itself covered in the shadow of falling leaves and petals as the morning wind stripped the trees bare. Two men stood before an audience of some of the most prestigious men in the empire, including the Emperor himself.

The first man was a formidable bladesman of impressive lineage. Hoshi Okami was regarded far and wide as the pride of the Kobiko Dojo, the oldest and most exclusive school in all the empire. It admitted no more than four new students a year. Those Kobiko students were all remarkably gifted and skilled warriors in their own right, and they required not only one but two letters of recommendation from the most venerable Senseis in the empire before they could even petition for admittance.

Above any living practitioner, and arguably any practitioner of the Kobiko art who had ever lived, Hoshi Okami stood a paragon of the way of the warrior. To date, he had never declined a challenge and had fought precisely two hundred and eleven duels, winning each and every one of them. He was about to fight his two hundred and twelfth. Hoshi Okami currently served as the bodyguard and principle advisor to General Aiko Mastay. Okami's opponent, and the second man before the gathered audience, was Kenji Rei, personal champion of the Shogun and Fist of the Shogunate.

Despite the prestige and station of the men involved, events had been set by simple indulgence of excess. Strong saké and even stronger words had passed the night before, leading to the unfolding scene that chilly autumn morning. The saying was, "A Solider is at his worst when he is without a war to fight," and General Aiko Mastay was a prime example of that wisdom. The empire had enjoyed an unpredicted decade of peace, and without the call of battle, Aiko Mastay turned to drinking to pass the time.

Sadly, as disciplined as the General was when sober, he was equally belligerent when intoxicated. Akio Mastay had been called upon to dine at the palace with the Emperor, several dozen other dignitaries, and men of means and standing in honor of his twenty-fifth year of military service. The evening had almost immediately become a disaster as the General arrived at the feast well into his cups and remarkably loose of tongue.

What had started as some well-mannered boasting, bragging, and humor at the expense of others had quickly turned into spiteful slander, accusations, and direct threats. Nobody could clearly remember what had been the specific grievance to break the good spirit of the evening—likely some inferred measure of cowardice or impropriety launched by General Akio Mastay and aimed at the Shogun. In the end, both parties had claimed a slight upon their honor which no apology nor act of contrition could amend. The only thing to resolve the incident was a test of martial valor. The terms of the duel were quickly negotiated, as both the General and the Shogun were eager to assuage any doubt over their honor. The fact that they each commanded the lives of one of the greatest warriors throughout the land all but wrote the story itself.

Many duels were fought over a matter of honor, and the custom was for both the accused and offended party to represent themselves. However, it was not particularly uncommon among men of standing to have a personal champion for their duels. Both General Akio Mastay and the Shogun were confident that the men they each had selected would claim victory and honor for their house and station. Word of the duel had spread the instant the terms were set, and several men had ridden in that very morning to witness what promised to be the greatest contest in several lifetimes.

Among the stone garden of smooth, white river pebbles, the two contestants stood. To the left of the Emperor's guests and spectators waited Hoshi Okami, who wanted nothing more than to serve his Lord as any loyal retainer would do. He had no specific feelings toward the nature of the impending duel itself, though he did recognize Kenji Rei as a formidable opponent. Hoshi Okami did not subscribe to every tale or rumor about the Fist of the Shogunate, but he had no doubt that a good handful, at the very least, had some roots in fact.

On the right side of the stone garden stood Kenji Rei, whose truest motives for championing the Shogun were a secret to all; the trappings of duty and honor were useful aids from time to time. While many marveled at the man's selfless devotion to the Shogun, loyalty and servitude had little to do with Kenji Rei's willingness to put himself in harm's way. His station as the Personal Champion of the Shogun frequently offered the opportunity to test himself against some of the most remarkable warriors to draw breath. Admittedly, Hoshi Okami was a warrior upon whom Kenji Rei had been eager to draw steel, and the good General's transgressions the previous night had granted him his wish.

It had been some months, nearing a full year, in fact, since

Kenji had experienced the pleasure he took in fighting a renowned warrior to the death. The last man he cut down had been Taka Shodu, a well-regarded spearman. Kenji couldn't remember what exactly had brought Taka Shodu across his path, only that his entrance was as swift as his exit. He had separated the man's legs from his body before neatly slicing his skull from dome to chin. Taka Shodu never stood a chance against the Fist of the Shogunate. This was a condition to which Kenji Rei had sadly grown accustomed. Despite the reputation and accolades of his warrior opponents, not one had been close to his equal. Most duels were over within three moves, and oftentimes less than that. Kenji Rei hoped that on this day Hoshi Okami would prove a worthy opponent.

The two men standing among the smooth white river rocks knew it was time to begin that which all had come to see. After regarding each other for a moment longer, they each offered a deep bow. Hoshi Okami held his bow only slightly longer than Kenji Rei; whether it was a sign of acknowledgement for his station, or a show of respect for the man himself, no one knew. Then they turned and offered a bow to their respective Lords. General Akio Mastay and the Shogun returned their champions' bows, though not as deeply. At last, the warriors turned and knelt to bow before the Emperor himself, waiting patiently with heads lowered to the bed of stones beneath them. After several deep breaths, the Emperor turned to his court herald and gave the slightest nod.

The herald was a dwarfish, rotund man with a jolly disposition. When the man spoke he sounded precisely as expected. "The Most Divine and Honorable Emperor Mako Tashanoshi the Sixth gives his blessing to the two warriors gathered here and bids them fight with great honor and spirit."

Kenji Rei and Hoshi Okami rose to their feet and fixed eyes upon each other. Both sported the twin blades of the Samurai caste. The daisho was composed of a short blade, the Wakizashi, and a long blade, the Katana. Most warriors used the Katana as a two-handed weapon, but several dojos in the empire taught the use of the Katana and Wakizashi simultaneously. A master bladesman with a weapon in each hand was a foe to be respected and feared. Kenji Rei knew Hoshi Okami had been trained in multiple techniques, and he pondered how the Kobiko student would attack him.

Hoshi Okami slowly and peacefully advanced to center ground, then stopped in a position of rest. His stance was poised and subtly crouched, resting the back of his hand on the Katana's hilt. Kenji knew the implication of this gesture; it indicated that Hoshi Okami wished to engage in Iaijutsu, the art of drawing a blade from its saya and striking with it in the same motion. It was an advanced, seldom-taught technique with a large contingent of warriors who vocalized their belief in it as the purest form of combat. Kenji Rei had a measure of fondness for the discipline and had engaged it countless times. So he advanced toward Hoshi Okami and took a traditional Iaijutsu stance before he too rested the back of his hand on the Katana's hilt.

They stood focused for some time, neither one wishing to be the first to draw steel. The greater honor lay in being the warrior to act in defense. In the back of Kenji's mind, drawing second was not a question of honor so much as a wish to meet his foe at the height of the other man's prowess. The Shogun's champion wished to give Hoshi Okami every advantage so there could be no dispute of honor in Kenji Rei's victory. Moments became minutes, and each man remained as still as the bronze statues of the palace halls. The autumn wind rushed through the picturesque display, filling Kenji's ears with a forlorn song. He pushed the simple distraction aside and focused on his enemy. There were whisperings and slight motion from the gathered spectators, who were also aware of the dilemma; neither man wished to be labeled the aggressor.

The Emperor's herald fluttered back and forth between the Shogun and the Emperor's ears, whispering some discreet correspondence between them amidst the impatient gaze of a sobering General Akio Mastay. After several circuits, the herald stepped to his usual position, hovering behind the Emperor's left shoulder.

The Shogun stood and spoke in a deep and resonating voice, befitting the highest military commander in the empire. "Kenji Rei and Hoshi Okami show great honor in their reluctance to attack unprovoked. No man could dispute such honor were they to act under the direct command of the Most Divine Emperor Mako Tashanoshi the Sixth."

The Emperor stood from his throne of jade and pearl, speaking with the power and authority of his bloodline. He allowed a single word to part from his lips and grace the ears of all in his presence. "Attack."

Kenji Rei's blood blazed with the thrill of war. No sooner had the Emperor spoken than Kenji Rei's hand gripped the hilt of his Katana, his blade flying from the confines of its saya. In a moment of brilliant white light, his strike was perfect. But the Fist of the Shogunate had felt no resistance at all between his draw and the completed attack. In the surprised breath that followed, Kenji Rei wondered if perhaps he had missed his target, or if Hoshi Okami had been quick enough to evade the blow.

He soon comprehended the situation as his eyes wandered down to the bed of white river stones, now stained red. Hoshi Okami lay sliced perfectly in two pieces, his face frozen in a blank mask of death. Blood flowed freely from the hollow of the man's chest and remaining stump, still attached to what had been his lower body. For Kenji Rei, the horror was not in the bloodied ground, nor in the grotesque remnants of what had once been another man. What horrified him was the position of Hoshi Okami's Katana. In the time it had taken Kenji Rei to draw and execute his strike, General Akio Mastay's Personal Champion had not managed to clear his saya—not even a half-draw of his blade.

The Emperor's garden fell utterly silent, but Kenji Rei's ears pounded with a deafening rush. It was the echo of fury and disappointment, resounding like the beating of one hundred drums. Hoshi Okami was one of the greatest warriors in the Empire, so it was said. And Kenji Rei had dispatched him without contest. A touch of despair took hold of his spirit as he stood there.

There must be a warrior on this earth closer to my own skill than this shameful excuse, Kenji thought. If Hoshi Okami was truly the second-best, Kenji may not ever exhibit the full measure of his prowess. His honor would suffer for that. He knew he must find a man possessed of the strength to kill him, to meet him as a true equal, and then he would collect that man's head. His legend was not at its height; he had more men to kill and blood to spill. Much more. The world would know his name for all time, until the end of time. He was Kenji Rei.

Most Esteemed General Wrath,

I have been long vacated from the shores of Purgatory. My campaigns in the realm of men have been greatly rewarding and have seen the Praytos swell with spirits claimed by the Reaper's scythe. Still, my extended expedition away from my elder brother's court has been a taxing endeavor, and I stand in need of some respite. I eagerly await the coming of the sixty-sixth day and the glorious spectacle upon its arrival. My duties have prevented me from garnering proper assessment of those who shall stand during contest. I am possessed of only cursory information surrounding the prowess of the chosen. I have never favored a woman in the tournament, though this time I am moved by tales of the scarred witch's bloodlust and the whisperings of the raven-haired beauty's cunning manipulation.

I find it a nearly insurmountable challenge to ignore my natural leanings toward the poise and discipline of the Legionary. While he may not possess the might or savagery of some of the others, he stands above the rest as a soldier. Such an accolade stirs the fire in my belly, and my fingers long to clutch the hilt of my sword and make for the heat of battle. My only scruple is that I cannot distinguish whether or not his discretion is a mask for a coward's heart. We are of the same breed, and I trust your council in most things beyond all others. If you would do me the honor, I would know who you mean to favor.

Your Sworn Brother-in-arms,

Master General and First Horseman, War

Vengeful Ghost

Part 2

It was pathetic. Kenji Rei could not lose. The Fist of the Shogunate was untouchable on the battlefield, had fought the finest warriors the empire had to offer, and not one proved to be even the slightest measure of fair competition. Single combat had turned bitter and no longer set a fire in the Samurai's belly, producing a jaded and dejected man.

Years before, as he had walked the empire, Kenji Rei might not have met a man who could offer him a contest, but there was at least the promise of one day facing an equal. Now that he had traveled to the farthest reaches of the Emperor's land and back again countless times, he knew he truly was the greatest bladesman within its borders.

Kenji Rei had taken to facing multiple foes at once, an amazing feat to behold. The Fist of the Shogunate was reported to have bested as many as twelve men at once. Sadly, the concept of quantity over quality only held Kenji's interest for less than a season. He still wanted desperately to feel that sense of peril brought on by the risk of death. Some began to call the man reckless and arrogant, while others said he had gone mad. But even his critics could not deny that Kenji Rei was a deadly force.

In recent months, the man had come to resent his prowess. He wondered if his skill with a blade was simply a cruel karmic joke—to be the greatest, but to never understand the full measure of that greatness. The Samurai had thought more than once to cast his daisho into the ocean and retire to a monastery, but he knew that notion was idle fantasy. Kenji Rei could never live a monk's life; he needed the battlefield the same way a drunkard needed that next cup of saké.

The passion and rage in Kenji Rei had always burned hot and bright, but these days it had a different source. In the past, it was the need to carve out his name as the finest warrior. Now, his ire was fueled by the simple and rudimentary tasks which filled his day. A time of peace was the hardest thing for the Fist of the Shogunate to endure. If he had to stand guard duty for one more festival, he swore he would commit seppuku.

With the news of brewing tension along the borders of two of the empire's southernmost regions, Kenji Rei had honestly felt relieved. He hoped with all his spirit that there was real trouble and that the rumors of bloodshed were true. He even allowed himself very brief moments to nurture the thought of seeing a proper war again. Kenji postulated that the days to come would only bring bold words and bruised ego, but he relished in the potential to draw his blades once more.

The region to the southwest was governed by the Wantabo family Daimyo, Wantabo Hogo. Wantabo Hogo had a reputation for ambition and wanted to see his family rise in esteem. The Wantabo Daimyo was also known as more of a passive schemer than an instigator of direct conflict. The younger man who governed the southeastern region was the Daimyo of the Kotaku family. Kotaku

Mio was known as a loyal and humble vassal. Despite Kotaku Mio's humility, he had gained some measure of renown as a leader of men and had drafted several papers on infantry tactics with the wisdom one would expect of a far more seasoned general.

The details of the conflict between the two Daimyos were not fully known; most likely it was a simple issue of territorial disputes. These types of arguments were the most common between neighboring regions. One governor would say one of their ancestors once owned such and such a bridge, temple, pile of stones, or other landmark, and that the current governor of the land in question must relinquish it to the descendent of the rightful owner. Naturally, the counter claim was that one of the current governor's much older ancestors first laid claim to the desired object in question. More often than not, these claims were just a lot of hot air, cropping up between bored old men to keep their lives on the outskirts of the empire interesting.

Kenji Rei cared little for the simple arguments of the regional governors; he left navigating that sort of thing to the courtiers and magistrates. The Fist of the Shogunate was only dispatched as a figurehead, to place a high-ranking face among the party sent to negotiate the matter between the Daimyos while one of the Emperor's bureaucrats handled the politics of the issue. For the purpose of this mission, Kenji Rei was simply a name and a pair of blades. The Samurai lamented the thing to which he had been reduced as the diplomatic caravan marched south.

Kenji Rei's convoy had rested at Tiki Hikige the night before, the last major city before entering the Kotaku family's region. The Fist of the Shogunate was anxious to reach their destination; he despised travel. Kenji Rei felt it was a great hypocrisy, and it annoyed him that traveling from place to place required the traveler to actively do something, while simultaneously waiting. He was glad this would be the final day of the convoy's journey on the road. With any fortune, the delegation would conclude the first half of its journey by midmorning.

They would be hosted at the Kotaku family's ancestral home for three days, where the Emperor's negotiator would hear Kotaku Mio's account. Then, they would travel to the adjacent region to collect Wantabo Hogo's version of the recent events, after which both Daimyos would meet together with the Imperial Court representatives to find a mutually agreeable resolution.

So far this morning, the journey had been a quiet one. Kenji Rei was thankful for that; the man was not one for conversation, especially small talk. The Imperial Courtier who traveled with him was normally a very upbeat and talkative spirit. His name was Goji Tokimo, and he looked very little like the quintessential statesmen so abundant within the halls of the Emperor's palace. Goji Tokimo was quite tall and had a broad chest and square shoulders. The courtier had the look of a warrior about him, but curiously his voice did not match its body. Goji had a very small, weak-sounding voice, and Kenji Rei felt he was listening to a child speak whenever the man opened his mouth.

Goji Tokimo had tried on numerous occasions to strike up some pleasant conversation with Kenji Rei during the trip. The Fist of the Shogunate shut down any hope of friendly banter with a string of one-and-two-word responses. He was not disrespectful with his tone but instead stared murderous daggers at the other man whenever he broke the silence.

That morning, it looked like the otherwise jolly courtier had finally learned Kenji Rei was not the talkative type. Kenji had begun to dread another forced exchange with the courtier. He watched the other man grow increasingly dissatisfied with the dead, hanging silence as they rode at the head of the caravan. Kenji hoped the diplomat could hold his tongue for the remainder of the trip. He didn't know if he could keep his Katana from slicing Goji Tokimo into little pieces should he be forced to listen to another of the man's dissertations on calligraphy, or the comparison of Kabuki with Noah theater. The only thing passing between them now was the soothing rush of the autumn wind.

The silence was finally broken, but only by the sound of heavy hoofs on the road ahead. Everyone in the caravan could see the trail of dust left by three riders as they approached the Imperial delegation. Kenji Rei saw they were armed and armored Samurai. The riders' standards bore the mon of the Kotaku family. Kenji Rei passed his mount's reigns to his left hand while the fingers of his right found the hilt of his Katana.

He spurred his mount to meet the rapidly approaching riders. The Samurai wondered if the men were friend or enemy until the other riders slowed their horses to a trot. The rider in front stopped and bowed his head to Kenji Rei once they had arrived at a speaking distance. Kenji Rei could see the other man had just come from battle; he sported several bloody wounds and made a concerted effort to regain his currently labored and ragged breath.

"Greetings, Honored Kenji Samma. I am Kotaku Mio. My family is greatly honored by your presence in our region," Kotaku Mio panted. The Kotaku family Daimyo exerted an astounding level of control to remain so poised in the face of exhaustion.

"It is the Shogun's honor to keep the peace in the land for the Most Divine Emperor Mako Tashanoshi the Sixth." Kenji Rei returned the slight bow to the Kotaku Daimyo. "Tell me what occurs here," he said, having finished with formality and etiquette.

"Wantabo Hogo has launched a full offensive against the Kotaku region. He has struck in force. I learned he had been secretly bolstering a large garrison of foreign soldiers within his region, and I believe that is what prompted today's attack. I knew your escort would be on this road today, so I broke from the battle with my guard in the hope I could deliver this information directly," Kotaku Mio said.

A barrage of questions leapt to the front of Kenji Rei's mind. From what nation did this garrison of soldiers hail? What was

Wantabo Hogo's ultimate motive? How had this plot evaded detection? Had Kotaku Mio's speech been true? Kenji halted his mind before it spun out of control amidst the possible ramifications of foreign military action upon Imperial soil. The Fist of the Shogunate felt that words were not sufficient proof. "Show me, Kotaku Samma," he said.

"At once, Kenji Samma." The Kotaku Daimyo gestured to the other riders that they would be returning to the ongoing battle. The three Kotaku Samurai set off at a gallop with their mounts.

"Wait here for my return," Kenji Rei barked at the Imperial convoy. The Fist of the Shogunate turned his mount and followed the departing trio.

It was not long before Kenji Rei heard the sound of battle. The clash of blades and the shouts of warriors in combat were unmistakable. He followed the Kotaku family Daimyo and his guard up a winding path which finally opened up onto a grassy bluff. In the distance, Kenji Rei saw the home of Kotaku Mio. The Kotaku family Daimyo gestured to the field below, where the Kotaku forces were locked in a pitched battle with those of Wantabo Hogo. It looked like a fairly pedestrian battle—with one exception. The Kotaku wore armor of emerald green, while the Wantabo wore armor of blue, but at the center of the battle was a single unit clad in armor of deep purple.

"Are those the foreign soldiers of which you spoke?" Kenji Rei asked Kotaku Mio. He pointed at the small detachment, which kept several units of Kotaku troops at a distance with their spears.

"Yes, Kenji Samma. They fight as I have never seen before. They withstood archery and cavalry, and our infantry is useless against them."

Kenji Rei had seen shields before, but virtually all Samurai rejected such a device. Warriors within the empire felt a shield was a coward's tool. From what Kenji could see, the foreign soldiers fought with long spears in one hand and the largest shields he had ever seen in the other. The shields were easily knee-to-neck in height, and he marveled at how effortlessly the purple-clad warriors moved about the battlefield. Any warrior who charged the foreigners and succeeded in getting past their spear tips was halted with a seemingly impenetrable wall of wood and steel before being dispatched by shorter blades. Kenji Rei was amazed by the sight of a mere twenty men controlling the ebb and flow of a field of six hundred.

He suddenly felt a stir in his spirit which had been missing for some time. The Fist of the Shogunate wanted to take the field against this new and exotic foe. He knew the Shogun would disapprove of his most esteemed retainer charging brazenly into battle, picking a side without proper intelligence. Kenji Rei would argue that these men were outsiders, with designs on invading Imperial territory. That justification would be enough to spare him any resulting dishonor.

"Do you know what they are called, Kotaku Samma?" he asked.

The Kotaku Daimyo looked puzzled by the question. "I cannot be sure, but I believe they are called Praetorian." Kotaku Mio struggled with the pronunciation of the foreign word.

"Praetorian, hum," Kenji Rei mumbled. He then heeled his mount and road directly into the fray. He maneuvered past the Kotaku Samurai and cut down any Wantabo Samurai who came between him and the Praetorian soldiers. When he finally met blades with the enemy, it was utter bliss. They were disciplined and fought with a sense of unity he had never witnessed before. The small contingent of twenty Praetorians felt like fighting an army of a hundred Empire Samurai.

As The Fist of the Shogunate fought against the Praetorian unit, he felt more alive than he could ever remember. He had to learn more about this newfound foe; the Praetorian held the promise of the worthy adversary for which he had searched. After the battle,

Kenji Rei realized he no longer cared for the illusions of honor and duty; only one thought consumed the Samurai. The Fist of the Shogunate would seek out the Praetorian and slay their heroes and champions. This he swore.

For Kenji Rei, today would be that day.

"One day, there shall be a reckoning, and all that was set asunder shall be made whole once more."

—Life, Ruler of Paradise

Vengeful Ghost

Part 3

Perhaps it was the day the Shogun would finally grant his most loyal vassal's request. Kenji Rei could only hope. The Fist of the Shogunate hated hope, or rather, being resigned to hoping. For him, the act of hoping for something implied that it was not within one's own power to obtain that thing. That sort of helplessness heralded signs of weakness. Kenji Rei was not weak, nor would he allow any man to think him so. And yet, on this day, Kenji Rei could only hope.

Kenji Rei was a man with a renewed passion. On the day he first met the magnificent fighting force of the Praetorian, the Fist of the Shogunate knew he had found the kind of warriors for which he had been searching. After years and years of meeting lauded masters of combat, yet finding them so far below his own level, Kenji Rei had been enthralled with a jubilant vigor when he discovered that there was, in fact, an entire people of the caliber he demanded. The Praetorian were strong soldiers and mighty warriors, and Kenji Rei wanted nothing more than to soak his daisho and armor in their blood.

Every day since, he had craved to relive the experience of combat with the purple-clad warriors. Knowing one's enemy was a principle teaching in the way of the warrior, but for Kenji Rei, the Praetorian had become an obsession. He studied their weapons, armor, and tactics; he even delved into their language and theology in order to better understand these foreign warriors. But the details were only glimpses. After the head-to-head combat with the Praetorian, the Shogun had forbidden Kenji Rei from engaging them directly. It was said that the Fist of the Shogunate was too valuable to be deployed on the front line of every battle and that a man of Kenji Rei's station belonged in the general's tent.

He would never directly disobey the command of the Shogun. While he did not hold the level of respect expected from a dutiful Samurai for his Lord, he would not willfully invite dishonor. It was not easy for Kenji Rei to be relegated to the role of spectator as the Emperor's Samurai battled the Praetorian.

At first, the foreigners garnered a small foothold upon Imperial soil by serving as mercenaries and blades for hire, but that ruse quickly ran its course. The small skirmishes among the border regions only served as a prelude to a greater threat. As soon as the Praetorian had assessed the military capabilities of the empire, they no longer bothered with the charade of serving as hired muscle for petty disputes between Samurai Lords. The Praetorian then landed on Imperial territory in greater numbers.

It was not easy for Kenji Rei to sit by and watch the battles from afar. The Praetorian had quickly demolished the Daimyo's forces of the other regions with little to no challenge. Not until the purple-clad warriors met the most seasoned and veteran ranks of the Imperial Army had their advance been slowed. Even then, the Emperor's finest soldiers suffered more defeats on the field of battle than celebrated victories against the Praetorian.

Each time Kenji Rei witnessed a battle, the Emperor's

military overcome by the foreigners, he longed to step into the fray. The Fist of the Shogunate had little doubt that he alone could turn the tide of any battle were he to personally meet the Praetorian. Each order to retreat enraged him. He took every opportunity to attempt coaxing the Emperor's generals to position themselves as he advised, where the Praetorian might actually break through the Samurai's lines and charge the command tents. It seemed only a massive tactical blunder or calamity might present Kenji Rei with the opportunity to fight the Praetorian again.

This inability to fight his new enemy had driven the Fist of the Shogunate to make such an unusual request of his Lord. Kenji Rei asked the Shogun to grant him Musha Shugyo, the warrior's pilgrimage. It was an odd request, seldom attempted even among the lesser Samurai of the empire—a petition for temporary release from one's Lord, more often than not to hone one's skill at arms and war practices in solitude. But when Kenji Rei had inquired about his own release, the Shogun had been shocked and insulted. No warrior of the Imperial Court had ever made such a request. Kenji Rei had had enough sense to make his wish known in private, the court ever abuzz with rumormongers and tittering nobility. Were it discovered that the Fist of the Shogunate wished to leave the service of the greatest military commander in the empire, dishonor on his name would be the least of his worries. He even thought for a moment afterwards that the Shogun would demand he make the Three Cuts of seppuku simply for mentioning his desire for Musha Shugyo.

It had been a month since Kenji Rei had broached the matter with his Lord, and it was a tense period of waiting. When he had last departed from the Shogun's presence, emotions had been heated, though neither party lacked the resolve to mask their feelings. Now, the Shogun had summoned Kenji Rei to the Emperor's court. The message was only a single line and it offered no clue as to the Shogun's purpose for the summons. It may not have had anything to do with Kenji Rei's request, but he could only hope.

The halls of the Imperial Palace were dimly lit and particularly quiet. He saw only a handful of courtiers scurrying about, attending to the plots and schemes of their Lords and Masters. There were, of course, guards stationed throughout the palace, but they were as silent and unmoving as the mountain stone, ever vigilant in protecting the Most Divine Emperor. A certain peace and serenity arrived with the setting sun, and the still of the night helped to calm Kenji Rei's raging spirit. This was not to say that he was always at peace with himself during the moonlit hours, but when the world ceased its commotion, it certainly diminished the echoes of his unsated cravings.

Kenji Rei walked hurriedly, the sound of his footsteps along the long, grand corridors of the Emperor's palace the only noise to break the silence of the night. The colorful lanterns hanging from the ceiling's beams flickered, casting battles of light and shadow upon the walls as the little candles within flickered and burned low.

Night in the palace was a beautiful scene, the kind of thing master painters longed to illustrate with their brushes. The sublime tranquility of the dark and shadowy halls had inspired more than one of the empire's poets to compose verses of beauty and mystery, whose meanings were the cause of endless debate among scholars. But Kenji Rei took no time to drink in the majesty surrounding him. He only had one purpose—to hear what the Shogun had to say, and nothing more.

He quickly navigated the twisting, turning passages of the palace until he came to the Shogun's chambers. Kenji Rei stopped at the screen separating the room from the hall and gave a warrior's assessment to the two guards posted outside. Both guards bowed deeply in respect to the Fist of the Shogunate, and Kenji Rei gave a cursory bow in response. He hated all the finer points of etiquette, feeling they merely got in the way of most substantial matters. He knew he was not alone in his disdain for the prominence of ritual and custom, but those who shared his opinions were a diminutive minority. The guard to Kenji Rei's right slipped open the screen to the Shogun's chamber and gestured for the Fist of the Shogunate to step within.

The room was more brightly lit than the palace hallways, but there was very little of import there to be illuminated. A large table sat to the side with a rack of row upon row of maps and charts. Another rack on the opposite side of the room housed texts on war craft, written by the most brilliant generals and warriors in the empire's history. At the head of the room was a small step to a platform, upon which rested two stands for the Shogun's armor and a place to rest his daisho. In between those stands knelt the Shogun, patiently waiting. The room was devoid of decoration, not including the ornate, finely crafted armor of the eight guards stationed along the room's perimeter.

Kenji Rei bowed to the Shogun after entering, then crossed the room to kneel before his Lord, where he bowed yet again and placed his forehead to the floor.

The Shogun bowed in return before he spoke. "You honor me with your swift response to my summons, Kenji Samma," the Shogun stated in his brisk, militant voice.

"Thank you, my Lord. A Samurai must serve the commands of his master swiftly, or his actions are not truly of service." Kenji Rei raised his head from the floor. The Shogun waved his hand and a servant entered, holding a tea tray with a pot and two cups. The servant bowed to the Shogun and placed the tray between the two men.

"Drink tea with me before we speak, Rei-San." The Shogun's tone was softer than Kenji Rei was accustomed to hearing. The Shogun gestured to the servant, who then poured and served the tea. The men sat, silently holding their steaming cups, and took a moment to reflect on their thoughts before raising the hot beverage to their lips. Kenji Rei longed for this formality to be over so he might know the Shogun's purpose.

"I have commanded you to appear before me because I have come to a decision about your request for Musha Shugyo."

Kenji Rei felt his skin burn with the heat of anticipation, like that of two lovers before their lips connect for the first time. He willed the Shogun to continue. Those last few moments of uncertainty were the most testing of all to which the Fist of the Shogunate had been subjected since his request for the warrior's pilgrimage.

"I shall grant you the release that you need, Kenji Samma," the Shogun continued. His voice was cold and detached, but the Shogun's words made Kenji Rei's blood boil hot at the prospect.

"Thank you, my Lord. You are most generous," he said. All he could think was how quickly he would make for the Praetorian battlefront. Perhaps he would even leave the empire, journey to whatever land from which the Praetorian hailed. Surely the native ground of the purple-cloaked warriors would be a magnificent sight and a world filled with the sort of men Kenji Rei longed to battle. He became aware again of the Shogun's expression.

The older man held his breath in thought, and it was clear he had more to say on the matter. "It is not so simple as that, Rei-San," the Shogun said. "I know that your purpose for Musha Shugyo was to battle the Praetorian."

"Yes, my Lord. They are powerful warriors, and I would see my own prowess pitted against them," Kenji Rei said.

"That will not be possible." The Shogun's voice was flat and emotionless.

Kenji Rei felt as though he had fallen into a pit at the sound of those words. The promise of feeding his craving, only to have it immediately revoked, was too heavy a blow. "I do not understand your meaning, my Lord," he said through a tight jaw.

"We no longer are to engage in battle with the Praetorian. The Most Divine Emperor in all his wisdom has seen there is nothing to be gained from warring with the foreigners, but an alliance would prove ever fruitful. The Praetorian feel the same." Kenji Rei's heartbeat exploded in his ears, the Shogun's words like thunder within a great storm. "There will be no opportunities for you to fight against them. They are now friends to the empire," the Shogun finished. There was silence between the Shogun and his retainer for a full seven breaths.

"I will not question the wisdom of our Most Divine Emperor. However, if this is the case, and the Praetorian are to be united with the empire, then I will no longer require the privilege of Musha Shugyo. I withdraw my request, if it pleases you, my Lord." Kenji Rei bowed to his master. He felt as though he had been stabbed deep in his belly by a jagged spear. The words of peace were not easy to speak when the call of war had been within reach.

"It would please me to keep the service of my greatest vassal. Regrettably, I cannot do this either, Rei-San," said the Shogun.

"What ends my service to you, my Lord?" Kenji asked in surprise. There were again a full seven breaths of silence, but this time it was the Shogun who waited to speak. Kenji Rei knew the other man was not searching for the words; clearly, he knew exactly what he intended to say.

"It is you, Kenji Samma," he said. Heavy tension hung in the empty space between them. Such a statement could end a man's life. Kenji Rei felt his fingertips tingling with a numbness that was new to him. "I may trust your loyalty today, but I cannot be so sure that it will hold in the days to come." The guards positioned around the room shifted with the palpable unease, the silent observers in the Shogun's chamber.

"I must apologize and beg your forgiveness for ever giving you cause to doubt my loyalty, my Lord." Kenji Rei nearly choked on the rancid words of humility as they fell from his mouth. His hands and wrists now echoed the cold tingling in his fingertips.

"Your strength is legend, Rei-San, but not without cost. I have seen the price your spirit pays for your prowess every time you step upon the battlefield. There is a magnificent demon residing in your bones. It is a murderous, vicious thing that makes you a great killer of men. You control it, for now, but this empire cannot risk the ramifications were your baser nature unleashed. The Praetorian alliance is too valuable to be lost to rampant bloodlust." The Shogun's tone bordered on accusation.

Kenji Rei felt his head swirl; he knew the Shogun spoke the truth, but it did not soften the blow of such a direct confrontation with reality. He could barely feel his arms now, and he noted the feeling taking root in his chest. A cold sweat formed on his brow, and he tried to think of how best to phrase his next response. "If I am to be released from your service, then what is to stop me from meeting the Praetorian of my own accord?"

The Shogun looked to his guards before he addressed Kenji Rei. "You misunderstand the release I grant you. It is not from my service, but from the living world. You will not leave this room alive, Kenji-Samma."

"You think a simple eight fearful men will stop me?" Kenji Rei said venomously as he looked to the guards and then back to the Shogun. He felt ice-cold.

"No, I do not think they will stop you," the Shogun stated. "What will stop you is the poison Master Motokumo Tamitaka placed in your cup."

Kenji tried to stand, but he felt so cold—cold beyond cold. His body would not obey his commands, and he could barely keep his eyes open. He felt the flame of his life fading, weaker than a candle's glow. This was not the end he would accept. He was a man of greater destiny. He was the greatest warrior who ever lived. He was Kenji Rei. Though what the man was meant to be would never come to pass in this life.

"It will be painless and swift. You shall go to sleep," the Shogun said. Kenji Rei had slumped to one side, his skin the color of the winter's snow. The Shogun felt the pang of mourning to see the end of such a warrior. What had once been Kenji Rei was now only a lifeless husk of cold flesh and colder blood. "Take his body from here, discreetly, and make sure it is never found." The eight guards made ready to transport the corpse of Kenji Rei

"Even if his head should be cut off, a warrior's resolve should leave him to perform one final act with absolute certainty. In this way, he shall become a vengeful ghost," came the voice of Kenji Rei, reciting a principle line of the Samurai's Code. Kenji Rei's crumpled form rose from the floor where he lay still and breathless just moments ago. The other men in the room watched in total disbelief, and those were the last words any of them would ever hear.

Kenji Rei's hands were as fast in death as they ever were in life. The twin blades of his daisho exploded from their sayas, and the Shogun's body fell to the floor in three separate pieces, soon followed by the bodies of two of his guards. The remaining six men had little time to react. Kenji Rei easily defended the attacks of his next four victims before the blades of the final two guards struck home in his heart. As Kenji Rei fell to the floor once again, he delivered final blows with each blade in hand to send the last two guards to the blood-soaked floor underfoot.

He lay still. In the dead of the night, amid the bodies of enemies, the Reaper came to collect the Samurai and bring Kenji Rei to a world of nightmares and death. The demon that would be Kenji Rei had only just been born.

...And so shall it be, that the Name of Greed be granted the title of Count and twice the domain in Purgatory as the six other Names. In exchange, the domain of Greed shall be accountable for filling the Praytos with twice the number of condemned spirits as the six other Names...

—Excerpt from the Treaty of Greed

Sacrifice

Part 1

It was nearly time. Time for the High Priestess of Blood to speak. Time for her to name her successor. Time to appease the appetite of The Burning One. Time for Shiva to take what was hers to take.

Shiva was only a third-year handmaiden of the High Priestess, but the whole of The Burning One's children knew that the High Priestess showed her great favor. The woman's piety was unshakable, and the frenzy which overtook her in the heat of battle was a powerful sight to behold. It was clear that The Burning One had touched the blood of Shiva.

Two other handmaidens had been named as hopefuls, but even combined, these women did not have as many war scars as Shiva. She was always at the vanguard of the defense whenever the Metal-Clad launched an attack on one of The Burning One's temples. The Burning One demanded the blood of his children once a moon, but Shiva offered her own blood as sacrament, directly to the mouth of The Burning One, no less than three times a moon.

In the barren chamber, the three handmaidens waited for the summons of the High Priestess. The room in which they waited was rarely used, and it lacked all semblance of adornment. There were only four long, carved stones, fashioned into simple benches, and Shiva and the two other women knelt silently, consumed in prayer. Shiva asked The Burning One for the strength to meet the trial soon to come.

She covertly looked over the skin on her arms and legs. There were so many scars, more marred flesh upon her body than fair skin. Shiva could account for each and every wound; most were inflicted by her own hand, but the Metal-Clad had carved a good number of them into her hide—her badges of honor. The one scar neither received in battle nor by her own hand was the same as upon the two other handmaidens. It was a long, straight, vertical line over the heart, a mark from the High Priestess to each of The Burning One's acolytes on the first day of their devotion.

Shiva recounted the birth of that scar as she ran her chapped, calloused fingers down the full length of the mark, over and over. The temple had smelled of smoke and fire on that day, as it did now. She remembered the red body paint of the High Priestess and the copper colored robes of ritual the woman had worn. She remembered the zealous sparkle in the older woman's eyes as she spoke the words of initiation. The memories were all as vivid as that first day—the short gasp of surprise and pain from the girl who had been cut before her; wondering if the High Priestess might burst into laughter; the gleam of the curved dagger which had made the scar; the cold feel of it as it pierced her skin and parted her flesh.

When the blade had first sliced into her, there was a moment of shock. Shiva had never been cut like that before. But the shock only lasted a moment, followed by the pain striking her even before the High Priestess had finished with the full length of the cut. It stung Shiva at first, then it burned, shooting in rhythmic pulses like the beating of a drum. Wave after wave and beat after beat, a burning like the fires roaring within The Burning One's open mouth. Shiva remembered how the blood, too, had burned like nothing else as it ran down her chest and stomach. By the time the red trail had met her waist, it was as cool as a flowing stream of water. And that had been her initiation. After the cut and the words, when the High Priestess had moved on to the next girl, Shiva had felt that incredible pain change somewhere within her. From that day, pain became Shiva's pleasure—one she hungrily sought.

It was hard to imagine that her now rough, haggard body had once been so smooth, a lighter tan than the dark lines of healed flesh. She did not miss the body she had before committing herself to The Burning One. After the first scar, Shiva had rapidly fallen in love with the feel of caressing her own skin, once torn asunder and then healed anew. She respected her time spent in prayer and ritual, but she clearly favored the opportunity to collect more scars on the battlefield and to offer the blood of her enemies as tribute to The Burning One.

Shiva searched her heart and felt an anxious and present fear in the air of the day. She asked herself 'what if?' What if she were to be named the next High Priestess? What if she were to speak for The Burning One? Would she have the strength for such a task? Never as a girl had she dreamed it possible that one day she could be so close to the highest honor of her people. Before the fears could overwhelm her, she ran her fingertips lightly up and down the thickly scarred, ruined skin of her right forearm. Feeling the evidence of past victories always reassured her, and she was comforted once more.

Then she heard Hallow's approach. Hallow served the High Priestess as her Ritual Master; he was a powerful, muscular man with dark, burning eyes, skin as black as The Burning One's mountain, and many scars of his own. Shiva had often longed to run her hands over those wounds, to listen to him whisper the story behind each one in her ear. That pleasure was a secret fantasy each time Hallow came near, and she was struck with the thought that perhaps it could be real, should she be chosen as the next High Priestess. The three women in the chamber now gave their undivided attention to the Ritual Master.

Hallow, in turn, looked over each of the hopeful handmaidens before speaking. “Cona, Moonata, you are called to the trial first. Shiva, you shall wait here.” His deep, forceful voice filled the room. Cona and Moonata quickly rose to their feet and followed Hallow out without a word.

Shiva was surprised. She had mentally prepared herself to be one of the first two called to the mouth of The Burning One. She wondered if being selected last for the trial was a bad omen. Again, the fear returned to strike her heart, and again she forced it down with the feel of scarred flesh beneath her hands. She returned her mind to prayer, but it did not last long. She was suddenly aware that, despite the departure of Hallow and the other hopefuls, she was not alone.

“Do you fear something, my daughter?” The voice of the High Priestess of Blood came from some unknown place. Shiva’s eyes widened, and she looked quickly around the barren room for the speaker. But there was no trace of her. Without notice, the High Priestess stepped out from a hidden alcove within the stone walls of the chamber. She was painted red from forehead to neck and down both arms. The crimson hue ran the full length of her legs, visible through the slits in the sides of her skirt. Wearing the color of The Burning One, painted on all the flesh of the body, was reserved only for the rarest of ceremonies.

“I am not fearful anymore, High One,” Shiva said, rising to stand. Then she lowered her head in deference.

“But you were. They bring comfort, I know. The marks please The Burning One.” The High Priestess gestured to her own impressive collection of scars, those emerging from the waistline of her skirt to run up her abdomen before disappearing underneath the fitted shawl around her breasts and shoulders. "Tell me what caused you to be afraid," she said in a comforting, silky voice which belied the scarred and battle-worn body to which it belonged.

"The trial. I do not fear it if I am surpassed by one of the other hopefuls but..." Shiva paused as she thought how best to put her trepidation into words. "I fear passing the trials..."

"You fear pleasing The Burning One. That is not what he has come to expect from one as devoted as you are," spoke the High Priestess. This time, the woman gestured to the vast array of scars covering Shiva's own body.

"No. No, it is not that, High One. I fear that if I pass the trial and am chosen as your successor, I will not be strong enough to maintain that honor." Shiva's words were raw, honest, but beneath her curtness she still battled the fear which dug its claws into her spirit. "For all my devotion, I have never heard The Bunning One speak to me as he does to you. How could I hope to be his voice among our people?"

"You needn't fear this. The Burning One only chooses those he knows will serve him to his satisfaction. I think it best that you put these fears aside." The High Priestess of Blood paused then, as though debating whether to continue sharing the contents of her spirit with the handmaiden. "I believe you will pass the trial and be named the next High Priestess of Blood this day," said the older woman.

"Your faith in me is a great honor, High One," Shiva responded.

From the folds of her skirt, the High Priestess withdrew the same curved dagger which had given Shiva her first scar. "I have more than faith in you, my daughter. I have one final gift for you." The woman quickly drew the keen-edged blade across the palm of her hand and waited for the blood to flow. Then she gently touched each of Shiva's cheeks, leaving two elegant streaks of scarlet upon the handmaiden's face. "Now you and all who witness the trial today will know you fight with my favor," she said.

Shiva was silent; she did not know the proper response, and the silence between them lingered before the High Priestess smiled at Shiva and departed from the chamber.

The handmaiden was alone for some time afterward. She felt the High Priestess' blood turn chalky as it dried upon her face. Then Hallow entered the chamber for the second time.

"Shiva, it is time for you to take the trial," he said. He did not turn to depart as quickly as he had before, and Shiva could see that he contemplated speaking more. "Cona was not chosen. You will be taking the trial with Moonata." His brow furrowed, and he quickly clenched his teeth after the words were spoken. He looked guilty for speaking, as if he had betrayed some kind of trust. Shiva nodded, and the Ritual Master turned and motioned for her to follow him.

The trek from the small temple at the mountain summit to the mouth of The Burning One was quick. It even looked like The Burning One sat in eager anticipation for the trial. Above the blackened mountaintop crag, The Burning One blew clouds of thick, black smoke, the roar of the fiery blood which boiled within filling the air. They followed the path inside the mouth of The Burning One, where it came to a plateau. The air was thick and dense with the heat welling from the blood of The Burning One. Shiva looked down and saw all the way to the bottom of the mountain, where the blood boiled, churned, and erupted with sprays of molten rock and slag.

Scattered around the perimeter of the plateau were Shiva's sister handmaidens, the elders, and others of The Burning One's favored children. On the far side of the plateau lay the lifeless form of Cona. Moonata stood victorious and bloodied over the body of her had-been sister. She still clutched the copper sickle and buckler of the fight.

The High Priestess emerged from the gathered handmaidens and spoke. "We offer to you the flesh and blood of your child, Cona."

Her voice echoed through the roar of The Burning One. Hallow scooped up the body with his powerful arms, then cast her over the edge of the rocky ledge. The body fell deeper and deeper into the blazing mouth of The Bunning One until it became too small to distinguish from the swirling, bubbling liquid rock and earth below. Hallow approached Shiva with a sickle and buckler and handed the weapons to her.

"Your children Moonata and Shiva will continue the trial," commanded the High Priestess. Hallow led the handmaidens to the center of the plateau and looked to the High Priestess for the sign to begin. The old woman nodded to Hallow, and then the Ritual Master spoke.

"To the death," he yelled, and backed away from the combatants to rejoin the spectators.

They fought viciously. Moonata was larger and stronger, but Shiva's fervor and savagery were unmatched. The handmaidens swung their copper sickles wildly, and the clash of blade upon buckler rang throughout the mountain cavern. They fought as they had been trained to do, refraining from the temptation of pursuing an early kill and instead seeking to inflict a series of smaller wounds first. They twisted and bent their bodies to lessen or evade the blows of their opponent.

New cuts were opened on both women—cuts which would turn to scars for the next High Priestess and cuts which would never heal for the woman who did not pass the trial. Each cut sapped a little more strength from Moonata, but each cut opened on Shiva only fed her spirit. The floor of the blazing cavern was soon soaked with blood and sweat as the trial dragged on.

Moonata's stamina was fading, and she attempted a desperate attack. Shiva could have avoided the strike but instead chose to take the blow. She felt Moonata's sickle cut through skin and muscle and finally lodge itself in the bones of her shoulder. She retaliated by burying her sickle into the woman's belly and slicing upwards to the ribs. Moonata fell to the rocky ground, spilling a sea of blood, and died within moments. She didn't make a sound.

Hallow rushed to the fallen woman and checked her for signs of life. After the Ritual Master confirmed that Moonata was no more, he stood and spoke. "The trial is complete."

"The Burning One has decided. Shiva shall be my successor and will become the next High Priestess of Blood," said the High Priestess.

As Shiva stood there, suspended upon the rocks above the boiling blood of The Burning One, she felt the rush of something new. It was as if The Burning One had kissed her on the lips. Her blood was on fire, and she could feel her own raw power made into something tangible, now holding it in her hands. She had never felt so strong, so alive. Knowing she would one day serve as the voice of The Burning One shook her to her core. If this was what being named successor felt like, she longed to know the power of becoming the High Priestess of Blood. Shiva could not wait.

For Shiva, today would be that day.

...And those who giveth of themselves without thought of profit shall claim a magnificent bounty in Paradise...

—Excerpt from the Edict of Balance

Sacrifice

Part 2

A year. A full year since the High Priestess of Blood had announced Shiva as her successor, and still Shiva only served as a mere handmaiden to The Burning One. It was far more than unfair. No High Priestess before had ever taken so long to step down. In the past, once a successor was named, the current High Priestess of Blood would be called to join The Burning One, taking the final leap into His mouth within a fortnight. But that did not happen this time.

The High Priestess was as invested in Shiva as she ever had been, but the older woman's attentions had somehow become patronizing. Shiva knew she was ready for the responsibility, but the High Priestess continued to tell her that, while she would undoubtedly be a remarkable vessel for the will of The Burning One, her time had not yet come. The High Priestess asserted that she had not yet felt the call of his fiery voice. But Shiva was a prime example of piety, and her scars were many and long. How dare the High

Priestess say she was not yet ready?

Shiva longed to feel again what she had experienced that first day, when she'd passed the trial and was named successor. The sense of power which had taken root in her was indescribable, and every day since, she had felt it fading bit by bit. Now, she felt almost as she had before ever undergoing the trials save for the hunger to reclaim what had once enthralled her.

She had not quite come out and directly confronted the High Priestess about the unusual delay in passing the title, but she had hinted and made many subtle pushes to gather what she could from the reigning High Priestess' mind. "Does it excite you to think that you will be called by The Burning One soon?" or "How do you prepare yourself to take the final leap?" She would ask these things of the High Priestess when they were alone but was never satisfied with the answers she received. There was no indication that the High Priestess would be called any time soon.

Shiva's thirst for what awaited her very quickly took its toll. She barely slept or ate, spending even more time in prayer and ritual. Her sister handmaidens surrounded her in the early days of the successor announcement, eager for a taste of what it felt like to be chosen by The Burning One. But that attention had quickly turned to envy, which further led to Shiva's solitude. Shiva did not care—did not miss the closeness of sisterhood. In fact, she found the abandonment of the other handmaidens a blessing. She no longer had to listen to their girlish yipping and clucking.

The only thing, she found, keeping her from spinning out of control was the calm she felt in the center of battle. It seemed ironic that combat and bloodletting could soothe her raging spirit, but Shiva made sense of it. Fighting in the flesh gave her an outlet for the intangible anger bubbling within. It was far from the pleasurable flood as it had once been, but the taste of blood at least quelled her inner turmoil. For a time.

She was also grateful that the Metal-Clad had emboldened themselves in their exploration of the jungles surrounding The Burning One's city. They continued to land ships on the shore in greater numbers despite the harsh conditions of the jungle and the hostilities of The Burning One's children.

The Metal-Clad and the children of The Burning One had been instant enemies from their first encounter. The Metal-Clad saw Shiva's people as uncivilized and bestial, a people simply waiting to be subjugated. The children of The Burning One knew the Metal-Clad were blasphemous intruders on sacred ground. The battles of their cultures remained gory, visceral. The Metal-Clad had taken the beaches after quickly learning that committed expeditions into the dense and lush foliage of the jungle would end in slaughter.

This sort of stalemate had existed for many seasons now—the Metal-Clad confined to the border between the land and the sea and the children of The Burning One held captive within their own city. But the tides were turning. The Metal-Clad had found a familiarity with the jungle, succeeding in some miniscule amount of scouting within the cover of the trees where daylight struggled to pierce through canopy. The Metal-Clad had come to anticipate the snares, pitfalls, and ambush tactics used by their foe. Small skirmishes in the paths of winding vines and streams were much more commonplace now and almost an expected daily occurrence. Shiva found the new status quo to her liking. It gave her some small measure of comfort to think that she needn't travel far to find a victim for her sickle.

She made her way to one of The Burning One's smaller temples near the outskirts of the jungle, leading several other handmaidens and a few porters to resupply the temple with fresh food and water. The handmaidens came for a new rotation in tending to the temple every fortnight. This was not how Shiva had pictured her time spent as named successor; simple tasks like this were far beneath her station. Her only enjoyment from these expeditions was a respite from the company of the High Priestess and the woman's increasingly unbearable airs. Shiva longed for a sighting of the Metal-Clad. The pounding of her heart, coursing with battle lust, was the closet she came to that momentary feeling of power on the day of the trial. Her enemies reminded her what strength and power felt like, especially when she sliced them open and spilled them dry.

The temple was not far now. The light beneath the canopy of towering trees shone much brighter than on the path behind them—a sign they neared the stone structure which parted the obscuring branches above. At least for today, Shiva's hope of opening up any Metal-Clad had drifted into a dream, and she hated the days gone by without battle or conflict. So she resolved to spend extra time in devotions that evening. Perhaps a few fresh cuts on her shoulders and a blood offering could bring the handmaiden some peace. If she closed her eyes tightly and imagined hard enough, it might feel like she was being struck by a Metal-Clad's blade. If battle was not to be found, the illusion of battle would have to suffice. Spilling the blood of her enemies was a tempting desire, but spilling her own remained far from unrewarding.

The air hung thick with humidity. A heavy layer of mist almost always floated several feet above the jungle floor, and beads of sweat formed at Shiva's brow, rolling down her face and body before splashing to the leaves and vines beneath. The heat was sweltering, and most other members of the party found it difficult to hide the discomfort on their faces. Shiva always preferred the warmth to the discomfort of cold, but the unrestrained heat of the jungle was excessive. To be fair, it was nowhere close to the heat of the flickering fires within the mouth of The Burning One. But most of The Burning One's children spent far more time walking the blistering paths and pushing through the vegetation of the surrounding territory than in close proximity to The Burning One's mountain.

The temple emerged into sight from the shadows of the jungle. Soon, their journey would be at an end, and she would cool her parched lips with a long drink of water within its stone walls. She couldn't linger too long at the temple; she wanted to return to the city, and the trip was half a day in favorable conditions. Nighttime travel was far more dangerous and had to be kept to a minimum. She would stay just long enough to see herself adequately replenished to make the return trip without exhaustion. Shiva hoped none of the handmaidens returning with her would cause delay. She loathed her progress impeded by the shortcomings of others and had no desire to repeatedly tell her sisters to hurry up and keep pace all the way back.

Something strange had happened, she realized, when she noticed no braziers burned within the temple. Several fires were always kept lit along the outer perimeter, but today there were none. The handmaidens attending this temple may have been younger and more inexperienced, but they would certainly not be so negligent as to let the fires burn out on their own. Wherever The Burning One was worshiped, fire must blaze. Something was wrong.

"Be ready. Something is not right," she said to those closest. They nodded in acknowledgement and quietly spread the warning through the group. Shiva thought to call out but decided against it; she wanted to get a closer look at the temple first. Even if it was time for devotions, there were always at least a few handmaidens outside, chosen to be the day's stewards of the fires and the temple entrance. But now, there was nothing. No movement nor signs of life.

Several handmaidens placed their hands at the ready on the grips of their sickles, fingers tucked into the handles of their bucklers—Shiva among them. A few women who favored bows had arrows notched and strings pulled to half-draw, while the porters with free hands readied their spears. Shiva felt her bloodlust rising, holding out hope for a potential call to battle. It occurred to her that there may yet be some handmaidens within the temple in need of assistance, but she quelled the notion for good as they drew close to the temple entrance.

Blood spattered the temple steps, smeared along the stones. Clearly, there had been combat here, and recently; the blood had not yet dried. Several marks had been made upon the foundations of the temple, and in some places, chunks of the hand-carved stone were chipped and broken away. Only one thing left this evidence—the weapons spitting fire, smoke, and hot lead used by the Metal–Clad.

Shiva caught the scent of death in the air. It would happen soon, she knew, and the anticipation of inevitable battle took over. She scanned the steps leading to the temple summit, where rituals and devotions were held, searching level by level for any clues to the story of what had happened. Then she turned her focus to the jungle paths heading away from the temple, hoping to catch sight of either friend or foe. There was nothing. Perhaps she had misread the situation; perhaps what had come had now gone. Shiva felt the fires of battle cooling within her and she cursed the day.

A shot ended the silence, and the stone at Shiva's feet erupted as the lead ball slammed into the temple steps. Several more shots followed, and she caught sight of the flashes of fire from within the hidden shadows of the temple columns. The Metal-Clad *were* here; they had taken the temple and set an ambush. Two porters were struck by the shots of Metal-Clad weapons and fell to the ground, followed by one of the handmaidens standing next to Shiva. The High Priestess' successor took a brief moment to watch the tide of scarlet flowing from the gaping void in her sister's belly. It was beautiful.

Several more porters immediately broke and ran into the jungle while a few handmaidens launched their arrows into the shadows. The others looked for somewhere to take cover, scanning for any Metal-Clad close enough to charge. Shiva had had enough experience in combat against the Metal-Clad to know they could only fire their weapons once before needing a breadth of time to ready the next wave. She seized the opportunity to front her buckler and draw her sickle, quickly engaging the closest Metal-Clad she could find.

She let her bloodlust fully take hold. She darted in and out of the temple columns, moving up level by level and forcing her sickle's point through gaps in Metal-Clad armor—easy targets. The men she killed cried out in agony as she ripped open their flesh; the steel with which they adorned their bodies could not save them from her unbridled frenzy.

She paid no heed to the shouts and battle cries launched from both sides. While her sisters lay dead, wounded, or routed, Shiva pressed forward. She felt nothing save the pleasure of spilling her enemy's blood. Neither the cuts from the Metal-Clad blades nor the hot lead shots from their wretched weapons were enough to slow the crazed woman. One by one, the Metal-Clad fell beneath the Shiva's sickle. And then, she became aware of herself once more. She stood atop the temple alone, drenched in the blood of the Metal-Clad. She had slain them all.

As she slowed her ragged breath, feeling the swell of battle rage calm within her, she heard the sound of a man whimpering. Perhaps some Metal-Clad still held onto life amidst the trail of bodies in her wake. Instead, she found an unexpected sight cowering in a corner. He *was* Metal-Clad but wore no armor, did not dress as a warrior, and he was absolutely terrified.

Shiva would offer his blood to The Burning One just the same. She raised her sickle to strike but stopped at the sound of her own language on the man's tongue.

"Wait. Wait, don't kill me!" the man shouted. She did not completely lower her weapon, only relaxed her arm. She had never heard a Metal-Clad speak anything other than their harsh and unintelligible babble.

"How do you know our speech?" she demanded.

The man pushed his hair out of his face and stood, a little calmer and a little braver now that death was not a heartbeat away. "I know many things, many interesting things. I know what your…Burning One wants."

"Tell me what you know," Shiva said.

"You who have proven yourself worthy—it is you and you alone who will lead your people into a new era of prosperity. You are entitled to this. The only thing standing in your way is your predecessor. Do not let her linger in your station. It is yours to take, so claim it from her. You have earned the title rightfully, and it is not proper for someone else to enjoy its privilege. See the one who has come before you to the final leap. Soon, you will encounter the agent who will aid in your taking of that which rightfully belongs to you. He may appear as foe, but trust he is ally. Stay your hand and listen to all he has to say. And then, I will see it done that you reap the spoils of ambition."

—Regent Envy

Sacrifice

Part 3

Shiva had learned much from the Metal-Clad. It perplexed her how a people so intelligent and advanced could have ever been thought so base and vile—savage, even. The children of The Burning One were proud and devoted, clearly favored by divine providence; they stood above all other tribes in the land. Then, when the Metal-Clad had come to their shores on grand ships from lands far and unknown, speaking a language without discernable reason, the High Priestess at the time had commanded the heathens be struck from the jungle. Shiva, like all those who listened to the High Priestess, had believed their action against the Metal-Clad was the will of The Burning One himself. Now, she was not quite convinced the matter was so simple.

It was unlike her to spare the life of an enemy, but she was glad she did. It must have been The Burning One who stayed her hand—the only explanation for all which had happened since the High Priestess had named Shiva successor. The desires of The

Burning One revealed themselves rapidly to her, the biggest sign being that the gripping power of winning the trial had been replanted like a seed the day the Metal-Clad man spoke to her. Now it grew, and soon, she would experience again what she had on that day. The woman craved it, longed for it, and it would be so.

Deltoya, he called himself, and she found the man well-possessed of the knowledge he boasted. He had said he knew many interesting things and had proven his own words true. In the short time Shiva had known the man, he had shown her that the Metal-Clad were anything but heathens. His people commanded fire and metal—could use one to shape and control, the other to make weapons and adorn their bodies in armor. The man had shown her food from lands far away with the taste of majesty and drink which left even greater pleasure on the tongue. Deltoya enlightened Shiva to how sagely and learned the Metal-Clad were—how they used ink and paint to make their words stay long after they had been spoken.

Clearly, the Metal-Clad were not the enemy. They must have been sent by The Burning One to deliver his children to the greater life they deserved. This had to be the purpose behind it all, and Shiva would be the agent to unite her people with their glorious future. It made sense why the High Priestess had waited so long to take her final leap; the moment had not yet come for the true nature of the Metal-Clad to be revealed. The will of The Burning One now shone brightly in Shiva's mind, and she would make it come to pass. Her people would hail her as the new High Priestess for all she was about to do.

Shiva looked beside her, where Deltoya stood with several other Metal-Clad. The party gathered along the border of the fading jungle and the steps of the city at the base of The Burning One's mountain. Shiva had lead the Metal-Clad through the perilous jungle to her home, and soon, all her people would be liberated, rejoicing in the wonders awaiting them.

Deltoya spoke briefly to another Metal-Clad, a man named

Hector, but Shiva did not understand their language. "Is all of this your home?" he asked her. The man gestured with the sweeping of his arms at the impressive expanse of stone temples and shrines, eyes wide in disbelief. The man obviously had trouble comprehending that a city so great and expansive could be so well-hidden within the jungle.

"Yes, this is our home, here in the shadow of The Burning One, where he watches over all his children," Shiva responded with a proud smile.

"How many of his children live here?" Deltoya asked, his surprise from the secluded tropical metropolis now subsiding.

"Many. It is a number I have not counted," Shiva said. She felt some difficulty with the question. Nobody had ever asked such a thing before, and it was strange to see someone wanted to count the people who lived anywhere. Deltoya spoke again to Hector, an older man of greater size and girth than the Metal-Clad who spoke Shiva's language. The body language, glances, and tone of voice Deltoya adopted around the man indicated that Hector was their leader. And their leader was clearly dissatisfied with the answer; irritation came thickly in his voice then.

"Can you tell me this, Shiva?" Deltoya asked. "Are there more or less of The Burning One's children below us then there are men in our camps on the beach?" His voice was as gentle and soothing as Hector's was gruff and abrupt.

"From what I have seen of your camp, I would say there are many more of The Burning One's children than you Metal-Clad. Why is such a thing important?" She noted that her question had put the man off guard. Deltoya shifted his eyes and bit his lip slightly before speaking again to Hector in his native tongue.

"It is only that we have brought gifts from our home to show friendship. We wished to ensure we have enough, to see that all The Burning One's children are given a proper offering. You know The Burning One favors the bravest warriors. To that end, we have brought with us very special gifts for any of the fighting men. How many warriors do you have below?" He struggled to speak some of the more complex words, but the Metal-Clad had a respectable grasp of the language.

"The Burning One has many warriors below. Perhaps twice the number of men your...queen has sent to this land," Shiva said. She had only learned the word 'queen' a few days ago and had spoken it maybe once or twice, but from what she understood, that queen was much like her High Priestess. Only the Metal-Clad's queen was born of a singular sacred blood lineage, not chosen through the trials like the High Priestess; the queen also retained her birth name, even after assuming the mantel from her predecessor. In this case it was Queen Francesca. It befuddled Shiva that the Metal-Clad had two names for their matriarch, especially because there was never more than one queen at a time. But she was coming to learn that the Metal-Clad had most peculiar customs.

She wondered how they had such a reverence for the bloodlines of their people, and yet, she had not seen one of them make any kind of blood tribute. Most of them had vast patches of unscarred flesh on their bodies—so much empty skin to show devotion—and yet the Metal-Clad held steady their hands. It seemed a great waste.

"Twice as many," Deltoya repeated. "Are you sure of this number, Shiva?"

Shiva didn't understand why he spoke the question so slowly this time. "Yes, I am certain." Her answer was once again followed by a flourish of words exchanged between Deltoya and Hector. This time, though, the men's conversation quickly dissolved any measure of comradery, now carrying a tenor of disagreement.

Hector then spoke to the other Metal-Clad gathered in the clearing, seemingly relaying instructions. Shiva searched the face of the Metal-Clad's leader and felt foreboding rapidly brewing within her. The man had the look of a viper just before it unleashed its fangs and struck. Shiva's heart froze when she looked back to Deltoya. The man normally exhibited an expression of good spirit, his demeanor always softened by mirth. Now, his eyes reflected nothing but remorse, shame, and more than anything, betrayal.

Shiva lost her breath as the awareness of danger took her, but her realization came too late. She barely had time to feel the rock strike the back of her head before the world faded into hazy shades of green, then red, then nothing but solid black as her body fell to the jungle floor.

There were no dreams, only blackness. Shiva came to and opened her eyes to find herself alone atop the clearing overlooking The Burning One's city. Daylight had nearly vanished from the sky; she had been unconscious for the entire day, at least. Her hands went to the back of her head. Once her fingers touched her scalp, they reignited the splitting pain where her skull had been struck. On wobbly legs, she forced herself to stand and take stock of the scene. Sound was at first muffled and dull, but after a few heartbeats and a series of deep, cleansing breaths, her ears heard with clarity once again. And she heard first the sound of battle.

Looking out over The Burning One's city, Shiva put sight to the sound in horror. The Burning One's temples and shrines were under attack, several already having been blasted to rubble or set to flame. The Metal-Clad had returned to the city in force and now laid waste to all which stood before them.

Shiva had been the instrument of her people's undoing.

The Metal-Clad invaded, and Shiva watched helplessly from the clearing. She searched the city below for any sign that the children of The Burning One might have mounted a worthy defense, holding their ground against the onslaught, but there were no signs. The city would fall soon, and there was no hope to save it.

Shiva cursed herself for being so foolish. She should have ended Deltoya when she first set eyes on him, the way she would have bled any other Metal-Clad at her mercy. Now, her hesitation had brought the destruction of all she had ever known. She should have listened to her instincts, but instead, Shiva had let the promise of elevation and status cloud her thinking.

She glanced mournfully away from the massacre in the city and found the path trailing up the face of The Burning One's mountain. The Metal-Clad had not yet advanced that far. Perhaps some hope of launching a counter attack still remained. Shiva set off down the path and headed for the mouth of The Burning One with all the speed her weakened legs could afford.

She moved up the side of The Burning One's mountain with a driven swiftness. She was not far ahead of the Metal-Clad. The invaders had finally conquered the city and were now on their way to the mouth of The Burning One; she could hear them moving behind her in the distance. Once she reached the mountain summit, there would not be much time before the Metal-Clad were upon her. She could only hope that some of her people waited for her there and that, perhaps, her prayers to The Burning One could help turn back the tide of men and drive them back to their ships. She passed the small temple where she had waited to take the trials scarcely a year before. How greatly the world had changed in so little time.

The blasts of hot air filled her lungs and bathed her skin as she made it to the mouth of The Burning One. She stepped through the split in the side of the mountain and out into the space suspended above the swirling slag and molten earth so far below. Shiva's heart fell once more. None of her people appeared within—save one. The High Priestess. The woman knelt at the edge of the plateau in the very place Shiva had been named successor.

The High Priestess was locked in deep prayer, and Shiva approached her. There were fresh cuts on the other woman's arms—wounds many and deep. The woman was making an offering to The Burning One, and then Shiva saw the pool of blood surrounding the woman; some cuts must have opened an artery. Of course, these cuts would never turn to scars.

"I have seen this day coming for some time," the High Priestess said, her voice so weak it was hardly more than a whisper. "I just wanted to hold it off for as long as I could." The dying woman turned her head to look at Shiva, eyes burning with an all too familiar rage. "Your devotion turned to ambition, and finally to envy, and now you have killed us all." She spoke with a scathing tongue, mustering what strength remained in her body to stand eye-to-eye with Shiva. "You were once the living embodiment of zeal and piety, but you have long ago forsaken true servitude of The Burning One and his children. You are only consumed by what you alone may gain."

"He chose me on the day of the trials," Shiva responded.

"Yes, he did. But receiving the favor of The Burning One means he calls for a greater sacrifice. All the blood you have offered him, and all the scars you have borne, were of little cost to you. Your sacrifice was one of patience, and with your planning and maneuvering to speed your ascension, you have defied the will of The Burning One. He will accept your defiance no longer."

Even in the sweltering heat of the liquid earth burning below them, the High Priestess' words stung Shiva with a truth which made her cold—cold beyond cold. The High Priestess raised her blood-stained arm and untied the fastening at the shoulder of her robe. The red-sullied garment fell to the ground, and for only a single moment longer, the High Priestess stood before Shiva.

Then the woman stepped off the plateau and plummeted into the fires of the mouth of The Burning One below. Shiva watched the final leap and felt nothing but a mournful anger in her belly. Only days ago, the world had been so filled with the promise of great things, and now it had ended in flame.

A great rumbling took hold of the mountain face and the stones upon it, throwing Shiva from her feet. The Burning One roared in all his rage, drowning any sound or thought, and erupted in an explosion of fire and molten rock. The great mountain spewed scorched earth far into the air, raining down an inferno upon the city and surrounding jungle. Shiva's screams of torment were drowned by The Burning One's primal fury.

Amidst the incinerating smoke and ash of The Burning One, the Reaper came to collect the new High Priestess of Blood. In a desolate, frozen realm of bones and dust, Shiva would bring down a trail of fire and blood.

"How I miss my fallen brothers and sisters, those who were claimed by Purgatory on the day of the Shattering. More so do I mourn every Valkyrie vanquished by the Reaper's scythe since that day. Such a loss is a thing of true sorrow."

—Hetha, Valkyrie of Mercy

Legend No More

Part 1

Gemmell had been the greatest of the Valhallans. The Skelds had written more songs in his honor than there were waves upon the ocean. His strength had never been matched by any man among the six clans. His bone sash hung three times the length of any other warrior's in the four islands. Gemmell had stained his axe red with the blood of kings and emperors; he was a Legend among his people. But that had been nearly twenty long winters ago. Now, Gemmell was just an old man waiting to die.

The Legend cursed the cold. He hated how the chill of the wind cut through his cloak and vest easier than a blade. He felt cheated, in a sense. Against a man, Gemmell could defend an attack, or at least cut his foe down in retribution for any wounds sustained. Against the icy gusts of winter air, however, Gemmell was a helpless victim whose only measure of surviving her frozen assault was to pull his hood tighter against his face and add another log to the fire.

The fire only offered minimal warmth. Gemmell's hovel was

so riddled with holes that any heat quickly escaped into the barren, snow-covered wilds. The aging Valhallan rubbed his dry, cracked hands. The cold played murder with the arthritis in his knuckles, and he felt the sting of cold on his body from stiff neck to brittle back and knees. His hands always hurt the most, their sensitivity likely developed from years upon years of swinging the double blades of his axe—an axe most men in the clan could barely even lift.

Gemmell did find a small measure of comfort in his reflections. Despite his feet having lost their swiftness with the passing of time, the flesh which had become hard and leathery after years of battle and exposure to the cold, the world now dimmer to his eyes and fainter to his ears, Gemmell's remarkable strength remained undiminished. The Valhallan sat alone in his chair, watching the small fire burn as he partook of a completely unsatisfying breakfast of very bitter mead and the toughest dried beef he'd eaten in years. This ritual had been Gemmell's morning for longer than the man cared to contemplate.

He wondered where the time had gone. He couldn't remember exactly when it had changed, but his life today was so different than the life he remembered. He had been young, battle a thrill. He had sailed with his brothers and amassed great treasure for the Earl's horde, and he had taken glory, women, and the bones of his enemies. Now, he was a white-haired recluse with bad hands, living in a drafty hut. It astonished Gemmell how little he felt like the man he used to be. He knew his clansmen still toasted his name in drinking halls across the four islands and that tales of his glorious exploits were still recounted nightly, but he also knew in the recesses of his spirit that the man in the stories was gone.

The Valhallan's hands found the bone sash draped twice over his left shoulder and once over his right. His looked at all the trophies he had taken from fallen foes, mostly finger and knuckle bones, but his collection did have several stand-out pieces.

Gemmell gazed at the aged, yellow-and-brown jawbone

resting at his hip. That had been taken from a dark-skinned king in the lands to the south, where they had sand like the Valhallans had snow. Gemmell had slain eleven of the man's personal guard, and the pitiful king had met a cowardly death covered in his own filth. It seemed strange how such a proud tribe of warriors could be led by such a weak little man.

Gemmell then turned his attention to the rib bone hanging over the right side of his chest and the armor-clad westerner to which it had once belonged. That man had been quite larger for one of those Castle Dwellers, but nevertheless, Gemmell had looked down on him. That man had been a strong opponent, and it had taken Gemmell's axe three blows before cracking the thick steel of the man's breastplate to land a killing strike. The westerner's broadsword had left the Legend with a deep scar across his massive left bicep. That had been a great day for the Valhallan.

The wind continued its brutal attack on the tiny shelter Gemmell called home, and he only sat and watched as the flames of the fire grew smaller and smaller. He cursed the cold again, reaching for another log to put on the fire only to find his stock of cut wood exhausted. This was his least favorite part of the day, when he would have to brave the raw cold of the winter air outside. The Valhallan drew the fur of his cloak as tightly as he could with his left hand and picked up his wood-splitting axe with his right. He took a moment to prepare himself for the rush of ice before stepping out of his home.

The world was solid white from the rickety door of the hovel all the way to the distant tree line, where hints of green pine peaked out from beneath snow-covered branches. Each time Gemmell set foot in the snow piled halfway to his knee, he found a new appreciation for the small comfort of his drafty hut. He lowered the hood of his cloak; the man hated exposing more of his bare skin to the winter's breath than he had to, but it was a matter of necessity.

The cloak's thick hood kept the Valhallan's face well-covered, but it notably restricted his field of vision. He knew how easy it was to come upon a well-bundled man, and he vowed to would never be caught unawares by anyone, friend or enemy, who came to call.

Plenty of daylight still existed before the coming of dusk, and the snow had ceased to fall since late the night before. The weather was quite fair at the moment despite the overpowering cold. Gemmell felt the swelling in his hands the moment he set foot in the snow. His knuckles cracked and popped as he grabbed the cord of the deerskin-covered toboggan he used to transport cut wood. He heard nothing but the wind and the crunch of snow underfoot as he slowly made his way across the barren field to the pine forest beyond. In warmer seasons, the trek to the tree line was quick, but the copious amounts of snow made the trip a real chore in itself. The Valhallan swore bloody murder upon the winter and her miserable cold every step of the way.

His spirits lifted slightly when he reached the forest, feeling the dense mass of towering pines soften the chill of the wind. Beneath the canopy, where fresh snow did not fall as easily, Gemmell saw the tracks he'd made with his toboggan the day before. The giant man followed the trail until it returned him to the massive fallen pine he'd visited each day for the last few weeks. The man readied himself for the impending attack of cold, then shrugged off his cloak, immediately missing its marginal warmth. But the garment would only be a hindrance while he cut.

The ice in the air burned his lungs for a few deep breaths, and then the giant man set to work with his axe. Blow after blow struck the fallen tree. It was a labor, to be sure, but Gemmell did not mind hard work. At first, the Valhallan felt nothing, but after a few strikes with his axe, the muscles underneath his shoulder blades reminded him they were not quite up to the task at hand. The old man pushed aside the complaints of his body and focused on cutting and stacking wood. The cold abated as he swung his axe again and again, and soon the man felt drops of sweat forming on his brow.

Taking a break from the work would just turn the sweat soaking his tunic to more cold, and the Valhallan had no intention of enduring a deeper freeze. He forced himself to cut all he needed uninterrupted, even by fatigue. Once he had stacked enough wood to last him through the night and into the following morning, he quickly donned his cloak and gathered up the cord to pull the toboggan back to his hovel. He looked at the broken, splintered wood he'd just destroyed with his axe and felt a stir of anger. Once, he had buried his axe in the hides of strong warriors for glory; now the Valhallan buried his axe in timber to keep warm. He missed the call of battle.

The return journey always seemed more arduous that the initial trip to the woods. Fatigue, sweat turned to ice, and a full load of firewood served only as added obstacles while he plowed through the thick field of snow. The man did not complain of the additional hindrances slowing his return, but he still cursed the cold. As the giant man broke from the tree line, the sky turned from clear blue to a murky grey. That likely meant more snow tonight. Gemmell huffed and shook his head in disapproval.

As he drew closer to his front door, he saw he had company. Gemmell knew the man waiting for him outside the hovel; his name was Oolie, and he was the only clansmen who bothered to come see the old man these days. Oolie stood as tall as Gemmell but not nearly as broad in the shoulders. He had been a young one, little more than a boy, when Gemmell had first met him. Oolie's first voyage on a longboat had been Gemmell's last time outside the four islands. He had caved in the skull of a western spearman with designs on skewering Oolie, and the boy had taken to him from that day on like a loyal hunting dog to its master. Oolie normally came to deliver mead and food but had only just done so the day before last.

Gemmell wondered at his arrival. "Do you think I have grown some great thirst and hunger, friend?" he asked with a grin.

"No. I am not here to bring you food today." Oolie chuckled, and his eyes drifted to the lengthy bone sash twisting around Gemmell's body, particularly the chipped knuckle bones over Gemmell's belly which had once belonged to a western spearman. He did this every time they met.

"That is a shame. I was feeling the urge to drink more than half a horn and eat more than a handful tonight," Gemmell joked. "If you are not here for that, what is your business?" The massive Valhallan scratched his thick, smoky-grey beard, then quickly tucked his hands back inside the deep folds of his cloak.

"It is hard for me to speak of it, brother." Oolie's inner discomfort clung to his words.

Gemmell frowned. "It is damn cold out here. If we are to speak as brothers, let us sit inside by the fire."

"That would be good, brother."

They gathered up the cut firewood and entered the hovel. Gemmell set about rekindling and stoking the coals; the Valhallan made quick work of it and managed to get a few modest flames to take hold before feeling comfortable enough to turn his attention to his guest. They sat in the only two chairs at Gemmell's single table. He grabbed his drinking horn and the recently delivered wineskin, pouring a horn of mead as he spoke. "If it is hard to say, drink with me. Mead is fast courage, brother." He took a long sip from the horn and then passed it to Oolie.

"I did not want to come, but the Earl made me," Oolie said after nearly draining the rest of what had been offered him. "He said I was the only one to whom you would listen."

"What does the Earl want you to say to me?" Gemmell asked. The fire had come to life now, and Gemmell warmed the frozen bones in his hands, which offered the old man some relief. Gemmell watched as Oolie gathered his courage to speak.

"The Earl wants your bone sash," Oolie blurted. Both men took a moment to silently regard the lengthy piece of leather hanging from Gemmells body and the trinkets adorning it. Oolie then briefly gazed at his own bone sash wrapped around his waist—the meager collection of spoils he had taken from the battlefield. It was a laughable comparison.

"Why?" Gemmell asked coldly.

"He wants to display the bone sash of Gemmell in his drinking hall, so that all may know he was master of the Valhallan Legend." Again, there was silence.

"He was right to send you," Gemmell stated. "I would have cut down any other man." His gaze wandered to the gargantuan double-bladed battle axe resting beside his sleeping furs before he spoke again. "Tell the Earl this, that I say to him what I say to any man. If he wishes to claim my bone sash for his own honor, all he has to do is take it from me."

Most Grand Chancellor Gluttony,

At the command of the Fourth Horseman, I am charged with securing your cooperation in collecting one of those chosen for the sixty-sixth day. The Legend seems to have forgotten his place. He has resigned himself to a largely unfitting end. Winter in the realm of man is long, and my words do not so easily find his ears. I would bring the flames of past glories into his spirit, and with them the need to soar to greater heights once more. Yet not even the faintest spark of vanity lingers within him. The direct approach is null and void. I have devised a ploy to instead entice one who is close to the Legend. This will draw our intended into the reach of the scythe. This one in the realm of man I have already set to purpose. His ego needed little stroking, but I would see you spur your impressive talents to motion and build his appetite for esteem and laurels in egregious excess. This one will quickly fall to our combined will, and soon thereafter, we will see the Legend delivered into our grasp.

For the Glory of Purgatory,

Archduke Pride

Legend No More

Part 2

Gemmell took step after step in calf-high snow. He hated traveling to the village during the winter; the path never received any care. The Valhallan had risen before the sun in order to make the journey. Had he left any later in the day, it would have been nearly twilight by the time he reached the village below. The man's eyes were not as sharp as they had once been, and he would rather handle his business by daylight than torchlight. The cold was not as bad now as when he'd first bundled up and left his hovel. Now that he'd put the sun behind him, it helped to warm the giant man against the wind on the mountain path, stinging like nothing else.

He could not recall the last time he'd gone down the mountain. His trips away from his hovel were few save for the daily chore to chop and gather firewood. The only thing of which he was certain was that the last time he'd made his way to the village, he carried far more with him than what he currently possessed. The Valhallan had no toboggan in tow, no travel satchel, no wares or trinkets for trade or repair. This morning, Gemmell only carried his bone sash and his enormous double-bladed axe.

He had unsheathed his axe the night before to check her edge. Her last calling had been so long ago, when he'd cleaned the steel and sharpened her blades before he laid her to sleep. Her edge remained keen through the passage of time, but Gemmell had run a whetstone over her the night before for good measure. Then the Valhallan had treated the worn and faded brown leather sheath, using oils he had scrounged up from one of the dusty and forgotten nooks of his hovel. The next time he called on her, she would sing as though freshly forged.

Gemmell reached back and drew his axe from its sling across his back. He held her in his hands, her grip comforting and all too familiar. She was not as light as he remembered her, and that had been a bit of a shock when he'd tended to her the night before. It seemed unfathomable that his hands could remember her feel but his arms had forgotten her weight. Gemmell knew the fault lay not with her; she had not grown heavier over the years. His arms had merely grown weaker. He felt her, full in his grip, as he trudged through the snowy path. Every so often, he stopped and gave his axe a few swings from side to side. Each stroke strengthened the Valhallan and put him more in harmony with his weapon. By midmorning, with enough stops in his journey to wield her, it was if they had never forgotten each other.

The day wore on and he grew impatient. Aside from drying and cracking his skin and inflaming his arthritic joints, the snow accompanying the cold made everything slower. Gemmell had never been the type to take waiting very well. The Valhallan was eager to see the outline of the Earl's village materialize out of the white haze. The thick white powder on the mountain path made a trip inconsequential in the warmer seasons a massive waste of time in the winter. He could handle losing precious minutes to a fault of his own, but when time was snatched from him by the elements, he felt as though he had been cheated.

There were few things to entertain his mind while he walked the frozen path. He remembered younger years when he traveled on the longboats; there had been a Skeld among the crew named Fritz. The man would often sing to pass the time, his voice making travel much more bearable. Gemmell had always enjoyed listening to the stories played out in the verses of the Skeld's ballads.

Fritz had sailed with Gemmell for ten years' time before his heart was pierced by a westerner's arrow—or was it an axe blade from one of the other six Valhallan clans? Gemmell couldn't recall how Fritz had died; it was so long ago, and he had not been there to see the Skeld's fall firsthand. But he did remember that, since then, his travels had been much less melodic. The only sounds accompanying him now were the wind whipping across the expansive white sprawl, the crunch of packed snow under his large boots, and the feint clacking of the trophies hanging from his bone sash as they gently bumped against each other.

He placed one foot after the other, pushing onward. His mind inevitably drifted between memories of days past and his plans once he arrived at his destination. His fingers fell to several of the skeletal fragments hanging across his chest. A Valhallan without a bone sash was no warrior at all as far as Gemmell was concerned. Sometimes, warriors did take the bone sash of another Valhallan, but only after a challenge of single combat to the death. Rarely did a great Valhallan warrior surrender their bone sash to the Earl so he might place it on display in his great drinking hall. But sometimes, when that the warrior was crippled, infirmed, or otherwise incapable of setting foot on a battlefield again, it did happen.

Gemmell would not readily relinquish his bone sash so easily, even if the command did come directly from the Earl. The only thing of which he could be sure was that, once he reached the Earl's village, there would be bloodshed.

At long last, the white veil parted and the chilled Valhallan set his eyes upon the smoke trails billowing from the hearth fires of the village below. At the far end, where the terrain began to rise again, Gemmell made out the shape of the Earl's lodge. Even the man's residence held a pompous, judgmental air about it, set in large and glorious contrast to the cottages surrounding it. At the center of the village sat the bustling drinking hall, countless folk coming and going through its doors. Gemmell remembered the Earl's drinking hall always abuzz with people, but it seemed even livelier on this cold winter day than during the summer festivals. And Gemmell hadn't been around this many people in a long time. The news of the Earl's request must have spread far.

Gemmell continued his trek down the mountainside. This was always the most difficult part of the journey for him. When nothing else existed but the road ahead to occupy the view, he felt far more at ease than when the end of the trail appeared in sight. He seemed to move slower, then, like the road mocked him towards the end. Still, the towering figure of the fur and leather-clad behemoth and his equally massive axe plowed dauntlessly forward. Sore with age, aching from the cursed cold, and laboring to catch his breath, Gemmell still had reserves of endurance. The path may have worn on the man, but it had far from spent him.

Gemmell passed the outermost hovels and some smaller cabins of the village without being noticed. As he plodded on towards the center of the village and the Earl's grand drinking hall, he heard the all too familiar murmur he remembered from days long past. It was always the same whenever he entered a town or village—the hushed whispers and intense stares of disbelief. Nobody approached the giant Valhallan, but he anticipated the inevitable flock of onlookers in his wake.

Gemmell felt a stir of pride that, even as an old man, he could still draw a crowd without so much as a word. Then he picked out the unmistakable sound of his name from the whispers of the awestruck onlookers, and the pride swelled. Envy, admiration, fear, inspiration—all these things went hand in hand with Gemmell's arrival wherever he traveled.

He wondered how things would proceed as ultimately one of two possibilities—the first talking then fighting, and the second just fighting. He had seen it many times before when proud men were at odds. All the pretty words in the world could not prevent the wielding of weapons when strong men disagreed. Words might hold peace for a time, but sooner or later, blood would be spilled.

Many people clustered around the doors to the Earl's drinking hall. Just as many if not more villagers waited for Gemmell than those who had followed the famed Valhallan. He looked over the crowd and it seemed that, if there were any trouble to be had, it would not come from those who gathered here. The onlookers were mostly children, women, tradesmen, and merchants. Several among the crowd had the looks of warriors but were neither armed nor armored enough to pose a credible threat. If there was to be an assault, Gemmell's would-be attackers remained concealed elsewhere.

He stopped at the base of the drinking hall's wide steps. The two great doors slowly swung open and several figures emerged. At the lead came the broad girth of the Earl. His long, thick beard was streaked with more white than black, and his belly stuck out much further than the last time Gemmell had laid eyes on him. At the Earl's left stood the haggard, sour face of his wife. She had never been much of a beauty, but the passing years had transformed her into a soft matron. To the Earl's right hovered two much younger, pleasant-looking girls, large in the chest and with golden hair which helped conceal the vapid foolishness of youth painted on their faces. The well-endowed duo was obviously meant to warm the Earl's bed and feed his carnal appetites. Behind the Earl came the wide shoulders and chiseled arms of his personal guards.

More bodyguards stood on the platform of the drinking hall with the Earl than he normally kept. It seemed to Gemmell the Earl had also expected things to come to blows. From behind the corners of the nearby cabins and market stalls came more armed Valhallans. The Earl's men held their distance, but they quickly surrounded Gemmell.

The Earl looked thoroughly pleased with himself, his face set in a haughty smirk, and he waited for his men to finish taking position before he spoke. "I see you come to give me what I want." His voice was gruff and gravelly. "Even the Legend Gemmell does as I command!" he called in triumph for all to hear, spreading his arms wide to show the span of his power.

"Is this the thing of which you speak?" Gemmell called back, clenching the leather strap of his bone sash.

"You know it is. I sent that one to tell you." The Earl pointed to Oolie's face in the crowd of gathered villagers.

"Bone sashes are hung in the hall to remember great warriors who have fallen. I am still alive. What you want is impossible," Gemmell stated. The defiant Valhallan watched the Earl's face twist and distort into frustration and rage.

"You are alive because you just do not die! You have taken the final walk four times. You no longer go to battle. I will not wait any longer to let the cold take you beyond. I want your trophies for my hall!" the Earl snarled.

"Yes! I took the final walk once to each end of the map, and each time I came back. And she grows larger still!" Gemmell shouted, rattling the bones on the straps of leather. "I have not met a foe who could end me, so I no longer go to battle. There is no glory in besting weaker men! The Skelds will have to wait a little longer to write my death song." A few stifled laughs carried from the crowd at that last remark.

The Earl's disdain for the giant man grew with each passing moment. "If you will no longer bring glory to this clan on the battlefield, I will have your sash for my hall!"

"If I were to take the field once again, there would be no glory for any other warrior. Let the youngbloods make a name for themselves. Who knows? One day one of them might even catch up to me." Gemmell shook the tip of his bone sash with an antagonistic smile, hearing the sounds of more restrained laughter in the crowd. "If you must have my bone sash for your hall, you can have it…if you can take it from me." His smile faded.

The Earl seethed with anger at the rebellious man before him. He ground his teeth and clenched his fists, finally managing to calm himself enough to speak clearly. "You may think yourself too great. Much has changed since you went up the mountain. You are not the Legend you used to be."

"Then come and test my axe. I will show you how weak I am." He had not expected to feel his pride so easily wounded by the words, but he hid it well. At last, they would come to the fighting.

"I will take your bone sash from you, old man." A deep, rich voice spoke from within the drinking hall. The large figure striding through the doors stood beside the Earl. The man could not have been more than twenty-five but was built like a longboat; had he not stood atop the stairs, he and Gemmell would likely have seen eye to eye. He wore a cloak of black yak hide, a long hand axe at his right side, and a round, black-and-gold-painted shield at his left. The shield had a long, twisted wyrm painted in the center of its face. Gemmell could not be certain, but this man fit the description of the warrior named Blouter. It was said that Blouter was Gemmell's successor for unmatched battlefield prowess. Personally, Gemmell had never put much stock in the stories, and Blouter was not the first who tried to take up the Legend's mantel.

"Who is this one?" Gemmell asked.

"I am one of those youngbloods you so generously let make a name for themselves by leaving the battlefield. They call me Blouter of the fourth island," said the man.

"I think I know your name. Are you the one who wanted to be like me? Wait, no. That would not distinguish you at all."

Gemmell's words were again received with laughter from the gathered crowd.

"I stepped out of your shadow some time ago," Blouter replied. "Now, I think, it would be kind to put you out of your misery. You have nothing left, not even your name." The man parted his thick black cloak to reveal a long, winding bone sash of his own. No one could tell by looking, but Blouter's bone sash may have indeed been longer than Gemmell's. The onlookers gasped and murmured as all gawked at the assortment of teeth, knuckle bones, and the visceral trinkets covering Blouter's massive body.

"Nobody speaks of Gemmell anymore," the Earl chimed in with a smirk. "They all tell stories and sing of the mighty Blouter. Do not make an embarrassment of it. Just give up your bone sash and go back up your mountain."

Gemmell took some time to regard Blouter and his boasting. He could not let the arrogant claims of this overgrown child stand. "Those are some plain little things you have there," he said. "Are they all human? I think I see a horse bone. Did that one test your strength for true, little boy? Did you pay for all the charms on that sash or did you manage to swing that little axe of yours a few times? How may kings have you there? How many warlords, how many Earls on that little scrap of yours?" He pointed to several of the more prestigious pieces in his own collection. A combination of humor and shock ran through the crowd as Gemmell concluded his verbal assault. Both Blouter and the Earl were now clearly livid.

"I tell you this. I have a space for that clever jaw of yours right on my hip!" Blouter screamed as he drew his axe and tromped down the stairs.

"Come on and try it, little boy. Try and end Gemmell!" Gemmell smiled as he hefted his double-bladed axe from his back and solidly into his hands. Blouter charged with his black and gold shield fronted and his axe set to land an overhead blow. Gemmell thought about evading the charge but resolved not to take the defensive so soon. He tightened his grip and spread his feet for a lower center of gravity and greater swinging force.

Blouter closed the distance between them and Gemmell took his one chance. Were he to fail in breaking Blouter's charge, the younger man would surely send his axe into Gemmell's chest. The Legend swung his enormous set of blades in a wide horizontal arc and shouted. Blouter's shield took the blow, but such was the strength of Gemmell's strike that it nearly took the other man from his feet. Gemmell redirected the leftover momentum into a second downward strike which rang off Blouter's shield again. He pressed and pressed the attack, knowing that if he gave Blouter any time to close distance, it would be the end of him. The combat drew on in this fashion for some time, Gemmell landing blow after blow, Blouter enduring each behind the ugly visage of the wyrm on the face of his shield.

Gemmell felt the initial surge of the moment pass, and the advanced years of his body reminded him he was not the martial paragon he had once been. Gemmell's strikes lessened in frequency, though just as intense, and they sent the song of axe on shield echoing through the mountains. Blouter saw the older man begin to fade, and he managed to bring his own axe to bear. He made a few light attacks where he could, all the while holding his primary focus on keeping his shield between him and death.

The Legend had to take evasive action, no longer able to continue pressing the attack without reprieve. He would strike a few blows, then maneuver to a distance again while dodging the shorter reach of Blouter's axe. Gemmell now sported some shallow cuts on his forearms from deflected blows, but Blouter had yet to be opened. Gemmell tried over and over to slip his blades past the edge of his opponent's wide shield, but the younger man's defense was swift. Were the combat to continue like this, Blouter would eventually wear him down and win.

Gemmell had to change his tactics. Instead of trying to

maneuver his attacks past Blouter's shield to strike meat and bone, the massive Valhallan sent all his attacks directly into Blouter's shield. He tightened his grip on the haft of his double blades so his palms burned and his knuckles cracked; he felt as though his hands could crush stone with the strength of that grip. With no finesse or grace, he brought the full force of his brute strength to the forefront of combat. Blow after blow rang out, and soon Blouter's black and gold shield was warped and cracked by the Legend's double blades. Gemmell bought his axe down with tree-felling force and finally struck Blouter's shield asunder before his blades came to rest far within the other man's torso.

Blouter fell dead at Gemmell's feet. All who had watched the fight fell silent. Gemmell looked out at the faces of the crowd, and what he saw unnerved him. To a man, even his friend Oolie reflected blank disbelief. It dawned on him that nobody had thought he could have bested Blouter; everyone had counted against him. He realized then that when they'd laughed at his banter, it was not at the humor in his words but at what they felt were the ramblings of a demented old man about to die.

Gemmell had had enough, and he would yet again prove he was the greatest of all Valhallans. He gazed at Blouter's lifeless form upon the frozen ground and raised his axe once more to strike before stopping himself.

"No. No, this one is not good enough to have a place here!" Gemmell shouted as he shook the trailing end of his bone sash in the air. "You think I am not a warrior anymore. You think I am too old, too weak. You are all wrong. I am Gemmell, and there is nobody greater! Not now, not ever. I will show you a Legend never to fade!" Gemmell roared to the dumfounded villagers.

He would would show his clansmen something no one believed could be done. He would undertake a feat so great, its tale would last for all time. The Valhallan would see his name outlast that of any other. He swore he would be a greater warrior than any man could ever dream to be.

For Gemmell, today would be that day.

...Let this endlessly flowing fountain serve as solemn reminder of the tears to be shed for every spirit claimed by the Praytos...

—Carved into the Stones within the Garden of Paradise

Legend No More

Part 3

Gemmell was bound and determined to return to his former glory. After his battle with Blouter, he swore to show the rest of his clan and the whole of the Valhallan people that he was not a relic of the past. He remained as mighty as the Skelds' tales praising his name.

He had taken the final walk an unprecedented four times, now. The giant had returned from an equal number of journeys—the tradition meant to be a Valhallan's last voyage. He had traveled farther than any warrior in the four islands—had done battle with men from lands some members of his clan had never even seen. And it was a challenge, at first, to think of a single exploit to surpass his former deeds and place his name beyond reproach in the tales of warriors' mettle.

The answer came to him not even a day after Blouter's blood stained the ground at the foot of the Earl's drinking hall. The giant had exhausted his thoughts, and the impossibility of such a feat seemed his only answer. Really, though, Gemmell had known a simple solution had existed all along when he gave pause to the notion. The answer lay in the question itself. Gemmell would do the impossible.

Of all the wars the Valhallans had fought and all the lands they had raided and plundered, none ever stood against them save one. Equal parts to the south and west lay the Kingdom of the Castle Dwellers. Their port towns bordering the sea were a simple enough target for the Valhallans, but the massive fortresses of stone and steel remained all but impenetrable. It was said they had a massive treasure hoard—one to make the Earl's own coffers look like a beggar's purse.

The stories told of a people, ruled by a king who wore a crown of gold so big no man had the strength to lift it on his own. The stories told of a king and his castle, guarded by an army of deadly warriors clad in armor of black and white. Each of the king's guards was praised as a mighty enemy who had slain no less than one hundred men each. They heralded it an impossible feat to lay claim to such a well-guarded treasure, and no Valhallan had ever made the attempt to storm the westerner's castles. Gemmell would see that changed.

The giant Valhallan stood in the Earl's drinking hall and made his will known—that he, Gemmell, would take the treasure of the castles to the west and wrest the crown from the head of the western king. He would only take the strongest and most courageous warriors in the longboat with him, saying that those who returned from the journey would share in the greatest victory the Valhallans had ever known. And he boasted, above all, that those who sailed on this voyage could claim to be true brothers of the mightiest Valhallan Legend. In the end, twenty-nine other warriors from across the four islands and from each of the six clans answered the call to battle, and the thirty Valhallans set out upon the waves to the west to do what could not be done. They would take a kingdom which could not be taken and slay a king who could not be slain—with a single longboat.

The voyage itself was a treacherous one, and only twenty-seven of the warriors who had set out made it to the shores of the western kingdom. The Valhallans weathered two storms, the skies splitting open and dumping a raging tirade of water upon them as they rowed. Jagged bolts of lightning and the blasting of thunder ripped apart the heavens above the sea. Gemmell had only seen one of the three men washed over the side of the longboat by a wave as tall as the Earl's lodge. The other two Vallhallans lost at sea had gone into the freezing blue depths unseen.

This time, their landing at shore had been bloodier than ever before. The Valhallans had not sailed to the western shores for many seasons, and the Castle Dwellers had greatly bolstered the garrison protecting the port villages. Normally, the Vallhallans would have landed their longboat on the sands of the west uncontested, then plundered the shabby little ports while their villagers fled before the savagery of the men from the four islands. Every time the Vallhallans had raided the Castel Dwellers' ports before, the westerners had never even bothered to draw weapons in defense of their homes; they instantly ran at the sight of the terrifying longboats in the distance.

When Gemmell and his men tried to set foot on the sand this time, men at arms waited for them. The men defending the beach were more now than simple merchants and fishermen; they were trained warriors. These forces were not as elite as the black-and-white-clad men who had repelled the Valhallans the first time they tried to venture deeper into the western kingdom, but the soldiers meeting the longboat definitely had skill.

Arrows were loosed from the shore and found home in the

longboat's wood and several of the Valhallan warriors' flesh. The westerners even employed the use of shafts, set afire and tied with oil-soaked rags. Gemmell's men managed to smother the flames threatening to engulf the longboat with the threat of a rapid end to the invasion. The Valhallans let loose arrows of their own, striking home in the hides of the defending soldiers. The westerners' armor was of tanned leather and offered some protection from arrows, but after enough volleys, the dead lay far more plentiful than the living on the sand of the western coast.

The ordeal lasted some time before Gemmell landed the hull of the longboat. In the end, only twenty-five of his thirty set foot on the soil of the western kingdom. Once the Valhallans had made it onto solid ground, they put their superior size and ferocity to good use against the western soldiers. Despite the greater number of men defending the coast, those men were fast put down by the Valhallans' axe blades in close combat.

Gemmell and his men left the port ablaze behind them after taking any food or provisions they cared to take. The Valhallans meant to lead a trail of flames to the very doors of the western king's castle, and Gemmell wanted the king to know just who was coming for him. He wanted the king to send his very best and would end any man who stood between him and his quest for greater glory. The Legend swore this war of thirty against a kingdom would be the making of the greatest saga ever composed by Skeld or Sage.

Town after town, Gemmell and his warriors set flame to wood and stone after vanquishing all who dared oppose them. The might and savagery of the Valhallans was a thing most westerners had never seen before, and word quickly spread to reach the king's ear ahead of the invasion.

At first, the king only sent a handful of men, as he did not place stock in such tales of barely more than two dozen men comprising such an unstoppable force. He discounted the stories as exaggerated rantings of simple country peasants. But he was rapidly forced to reevaluate his initial assessment of the threat when he received a blood-soaked basket containing the fingerless hands of the few officers he had dispatched. He was forced to take notice again when he saw with his own eyes that the tales of villages set to flame one after another were entirely true. At night, from the very highest tower of his castle, the king watched his land glow red with flame. Once the king had seen for himself how these barbaric animals refused to die, he swore they would come no farther into his realm. He would see them wiped clean from this world.

Only six of Gemmell's warriors had fallen before this day. Most of the departed Valhallans had been so caught up in the heat of battle, they forgot they were men of flesh and blood; a fine edge separated foolishness from courage. Much of Gemmell's longevity as a warrior was equally attributed to his daunting physical prowess and his ability to distinguish an ignorant decision on the battlefield from a brave one.

In the fourth town they razed to embers, the giant watched as Hanaf, without shield, pressed no less than ten bowmen across open ground. The man died riddled with arrow shafts before he even managed to close half the distance. In the sixth town, Gemmell saw Brethel leap from a watchtower to land a strike upon the head of a spearman. He certainly cleaved the westerner in two, but the Valhallan broke both his legs in the maneuver. Brethel died trampled under the boots of both western soldiers and his brother Valhallans alike. Gemmell may have been brash, but rarely was he as reckless as the younger men fighting beside him.

The remaining nineteen Valhallans meant to set upon another small town and leave it in a shroud of smoke and ash, but that was not what happened. The town was devoid of inhabitants but far from empty. The king had sent two hundred and fifty men to hold the ground against the Valhallan advance, and among the soldiers sent were at least two dozen of the king's elite black and white warriors. The king himself had accompanied them to witness the destruction of the men rampaging through his lands.

The battle did not bode well for the Valhallans. Three of their numbers were laid down in the mud before any of them realized just how many enemy soldiers opposed them. Archers had the Valhallans pinned down next to an old mill house. The western bows slowly but surely picked apart the dwindling ranks of the northern invaders, and when only eleven Valhallans remained, most of them sporting injuries of some kind, the western king ordered his men to advance. Gemmell clearly saw the western king's men would overwhelm them, but he pushed the fear and doubt from his spirit and proceeded to meet his foe.

Now, only Gemmell stood against the army. After Ranek fell to the ground with the broken shaft of a western arrow lodged in his neck, the Legend became the last of thirty who had set sail barely more than a moon's turn before. He glanced at the bodies of his fallen brothers strewn amidst the far more numerous westerner corpses. The giant Valhallan felt a stir of pride deep within at the evidence of his people, the stronger warriors.

Pain shot through him from countless wounds covering his body. His advance across the western land had borne a trail of fire, and with it a trail of his own blood. He had to admit that the skill of the western soldiers was not to be discounted. At the onset, it had seemed nothing within the western king's land could hold back the Valhallans' march. Now, Gemmell stood battered, bruised, soaked with his own blood, and surrounded by a foe beyond his eye's counting.

He gripped his double-bladed axe firmly with both hands and held his position against the force encircling him. He searched the opposing soldiers and noted how they kept their distance. They had seen enough of his might, and even still they knew drawing close to him would likely cost them their lives. No western soldier advanced; clearly, their courage waned when faced with the prospect of being the first man within striking distance. True, the weight of numbers would eventually overwhelm any man, but everyone knew that the first to fight were the first to die. Gemmell glared at them, willing them to attack. He had expected some fear from the regular rank-and-file soldiers, but even the king's elite refused to engage in the fight.

Gemmell would wait no longer. If the westerners would not fight him, the Valhallan would bring the fight to them. He commanded his aching body to charge. Instead of the pounding of feet upon the ground followed by the strike of axe on shield, Gemmell found himself suddenly on one knee. He commanded his body to rise, but it would not, and then his strength failed him. The completely new, unfathomable experience for the man caused him to look slowly over his body, where he saw the cascading flow of red seeping from cut upon cut. He realized what was happening. The westerners were not afraid of him; they were just waiting for Gemmell to die.

The heat of battle turned cold as blood ran from his torn flesh. Gemmell cursed the cold—that cold beyond cold. This was not the end the Valhallan had envisioned, nor was it the death befitting a Legend—surrounded by gawking little men who thought themselves equal warriors. It disgusted him.

Then, his anger peaked when he saw the image of the western king sitting high atop his horse. Only now that the fighting had ended did the little man with the great golden crown come down to see the Valhallan. Gemmell knew the king would surely take credit and glory for a victory he never even raised steel to claim. He would not have it so.

The giant Valhallan summoned all the power remaining within his body, and with one final act of unbelievable strength, he hurled his enormous double-bladed axe through the air. The western soldiers gasped and cried out, but none were fast enough to predict or defend against the unexpected. The outcry magnified a hundredfold as the mighty axe sank deep into the chest of the western king, toppling him from his horse.

Gemmell felt no pain as he fell to the mud. The image of the little king split in two put all agony aside and placed a smile on the Valhallan's lips. His eyes closed as the breath left his body and his heart ceased to beat. His last regret was that he would never have a chance to take a trophy from the western king to wear on his bone sash.

In the mud and filth, littered by the corpses of fallen warriors, the Reaper came to collect the Valhallan. The Legend would rise to greater glory still.

"He does not know it, but I am coming for him. Many times in this one's life have I been close to collecting him, but always, he has slipped out of reach. No more. This time he will not escape, and I will have him. His spirit weighs heavy with gravest burden. When the time comes, my steed will thunder to meet him, faster than the beating wings of any Valkyrie in Paradise. I will not be robbed of taking this man to his deserved end, not by those who would grant him reprieve. I have waited patiently, and I shall do so until I receive the order of my master to breach the realm of man and put my scythe to task. Until that time, I relish each moment of anguish and suffering this man endures along his journey to the Praytos. With what is to come, I will not want for delight."

—Lynch, the Pale Rider and Favored Reaper of Warden Sloth

Mourning Dove Song

Part 1

He felt it flow through him, though he knew not what. Somehow, he knew a reckoning approached, fast and hard.

As the rising sun broke the horizon, the Marshal looked up from the smoldering embers of his campfire and allowed the first rays of morning light to greet him. He finished the modest breakfast he had prepared for himself; black coffee and boiled oats. Jackson Bennett French lamented the fact that he had to take his coffee without a spoonful of sugar to calm the bitterness but was grateful for the pinch of salt he'd discovered tucked away in his saddlebags. That gave the oats some flavor. The Marshal did not allow himself to dwell too long on the meal which left him wanting. In fact, he considered it a silver lining—a larger, more substantial meal would have made him slower on the draw, and he feared he might need speed of hand today.

Jackson folded his bedroll after dousing the remnants of the campfire and extinguishing any remaining life in the coals. Ghostly trails of smoke interlaced themselves in the Marshal's silver hair as he set about breaking camp. Putting his items in order was a quick affair. Then it came time for Jackson Bennett French's final and most important task of the morning.

The Marshal drew both his long-barrel forty-fives and broke open the cylinder of each. He checked and double-checked each pistol—six rounds in each and twelve rounds total. He checked his gun belt, and every loop had a bullet snugly tucked into it. Finally, Jackson reached grabbed the double-barrel shotgun he'd laid against the desert willow which had offered some cover for the night. The Marshal broke open the barrel and counted two shells. *Everything is as it should be*, he thought. With all his effects accounted for, the Marshal picked up his pack and saddle, making his way toward his favorite deputy.

Annabel was the best mount Jackson had had by far—a grey mare who had ridden with the Marshal for the better part of a decade. His first horse had been a temperamental Palomino stallion named Willy, who had taken a stray bullet to his left eye two years into Jackson's term of service on what was supposed to be a simple grab-and-go. But it had turned into a gun fight and bar brawl, blowing out the entire first floor of the Red Cat Dance Hall.

The second horse had been another stallion named Henry—a black quarter horse sporting quite the temper. Henry had served the Marshal for eight years before being struck lame one icy winter, and Jackson had put Henry down himself. The third horse, a brown mare named Elli, had carried the Marshal for six years before taking two loads of buckshot to her gut while Jackson rode down David Cass and his three brothers.

The Cass Brothers had been wanted for nearly two dozen payroll holdups over the course of only two years. David and two of his brothers had died by Jackson's own hands when the Marshal had cornered them in a box canyon, and the final Cass brother had been sentenced and hanged by week's end. Jackson Bennett French had come away from the whole ordeal down one horse and up a small limp during particularly cold weather; a couple pellets had cut too deep into his right thigh for the doc to fish out. The best part of Jackson's entanglement with the quartet had been his introduction to Annabel, the gray mare who served him to this day.

Both the Marshal and Annabel were early risers when on the trail. Jackson knew catching a fugitive was more often than not a matter of endurance; that meant a Marshal had to ride longer and harder than those on the other side of the tin star. This was not the most difficult track Jackson had been on, at least physically speaking. His aging back, hands, and knees were grateful for that small mercy. Morally speaking, this track was not so kind. Jackson never hesitated for a moment when it came time to run down or even draw down on a career outlaw, but the first-timers were never an easy grab, especially when they were not even full-grown men. This particular fugitive was merely a boy of fourteen named Daniel Bradley, and running down a boy with maybe one or two of his friends was a father's job, not a task for a Marshal.

The whole thing was one big, sloppy mess, and Jackson had known it would turn ugly from the beginning. He'd heard Daniel had gotten hold of a bottle of Shine and his daddy's lever-action Sharpe, then decided to go shooting with some of his pals one afternoon instead of minding his family's cattle pen. It was a miracle none of the boys had blown a hole in each other, but the same fortune had not extended to the Bradleys' neighbor's daughter, Maggie Foster. Maggie was only a girl of eleven, and she'd been riding her pony Sugar along the property line with her father the same afternoon Daniel and his friends decided to play with guns and alcohol for the first time. Nobody had been shot—the Marshal thanked the stars for that—but one of Daniel's bullets had missed Maggie's nose by a hair's breadth and spooked Sugar something fierce. The tiny girl had been thrown with a hard landing, breaking her leg and three fingers.

This kind of mischief wasn't all that uncommon within the

territory, and considering there had been neither loss of life nor wounds which wouldn't heal in time, a simple whipping with a knotted bull rope would normally be the end of it. Maggie's father was the sole reason Jackson Bennett French had been sent on this track. The man was a circuit judge and the most notorious in the southwest. Judge Foster liked to make an example of anyone sitting in his court, so much so that the man boasted of sending more outlaws to the hangman's noose than all the other territory judges combined.

The affection and warmth the Judge showed for his daughter remained the only evidence of love in the man's heart. Judge Foster had vowed retribution upon those responsible for hurting his little girl and would see them beg for their lives before they swung on the end of a rope. Jackson had wished this track had fallen to a different Marshal, or that this whole, awful mess had never been set in motion to begin with, but it wasn't that easy. Daniel and his friends had not made any effort, and likely didn't even have the mind, to conceal their trail, so Jackson knew he'd catch up with them this morning. Clearly, the boys were headed to the town of Tall Sky, where they could likely try to hop the last rail car of the week to go back east.

The completely flat area surrounding Tall Sky offered little in the way of cover—with one notable exception. Several boulders had collected over years of flash-flooding, resting now in a dried river bed about five hours' ride from the outskirts of the town; they made as good a campsite as any for those with business in town and a wish to remain unseen.

Jackson figured that, with any luck, he could catch the boys off guard and perhaps still asleep. He had been awake before the break of day and on the move with the first signs of daylight, and he would now have the rising sun at his back, making it harder for them to detect his approach. As the Marshal laid eyes on the rock formation, he slowed Annabel to a trot and guided her to the dried, broken branches and fallen trunk of what might have been a desert willow; it seemed the thing had tried to grow on the range once upon a time. Jackson dismounted and tied Annabel's reigns to the sturdiest of the willow's remaining branches.

He reached into his saddlebag and grabbed his spyglass, surveyed the boulders, and confirmed his suspicions. There were three of the Bradleys' horses tied off among the rocks; the boys were close by. Jackson had to move quickly but didn't want to rush in before getting a strong read on the situation. The Marshal saw no movement among the boulders, confident that Daniel and his companions still slept and had not bothered to appoint a lookout. His approach would place him between anyone camped in the rocks and the horses tied off on the perimeter, and he was grateful for this fact. It meant a mounted pursuit wouldn't be a concern and he could leave Annabel at a safe distance.

"Stay here, girl, and watch my back," he told the horse, the faintest hint of a grin concealed behind his silver mustache. The grey mare paid no heed to her rider, expressing more interest in investigating the fallen tree to which she'd been tethered. Jackson double-checked his gun belt and grabbed his double-barrel and a length of rope from his saddle horn. He figured he'd present an intimidating enough image to a handful of barley-conscious, frightened boys that they'd come along with minimum coaxing. Despite his age and the objections of his knees, the Marshal still covered the distance from the fallen willow to the collection of boulders with surprising alacrity and silence.

As he'd hoped, Daniel and the two other boys were still asleep. He took a moment to survey the rag-tag camp—which consisted of little more than a pile of blankets—and noted that the boys had armed themselves with firearms all out of immediate reach. He gave himself a moment to compose his words before speaking.

"All right, boys, wake up!" the Marshal barked with the veteran experience of a man who had years of rousing sleeping children under his belt. Daniel sat up like a shot, the two others not far behind. The three boys froze solid with the fear of being awakened at gunpoint.

"Daniel Bradley, I'm with the Marshals. You and your friends need to come with me." Jackson's voice was calmer but still commanding. He shifted his gaze from one boy to the next, making sure he could see their hands at all times. The Marshal recognized both the other boys; to Daniel's left sat Jimmy Thomas, the Blacksmith's son, and to Daniel's right was Harrison Bridge, who lived with his aunt and uncle. Harrison eagerly eyed the gun belt at the end of his bedroll, and Jimmy's gaze frequently darted to the lever-action resting against a nearby boulder. "Y'all ain't killers, and y'all don't want to be on the run. I know that, so just stay calm and move slow."

"We can't go back. Judge Foster wants to hang us," Daniel said after several moments of silence. The boy's voice was barely more than a whisper and filled with dread. Jackson couldn't tell if Daniel was frightened more by the sight of an armed Marshal or the possibility of what might happen should he be delivered to the Judge.

"Look, Son, y'all get a chance to tell your side and say your piece. Maggie's alive, and nothing happened to her which time and some proper doctoring won't fix," the Marshal said. "The Judge was angry and in the heat of the moment. He said some things in a temper 'cause he was scared for his girl, is all. Just come on back to town with me and we'll get this straightened out."

"No, it won't be like that," Harrison chimed in. "Foster will kill us. He swore he would. We could hear him shouting after us as we rode out." His voice didn't shake as much as Daniel's, but the Marshal heard the fear in his words.

"Boys, this is all one big misunderstanding. Your folks are all worried to death. Daniel, your ma especially. She just wants her boy to come home. Running ain't gonna fix this none." He tried to appeal to the boys' love for their families and noticed each of them in turn fixating on the guns scattered about their camp. He watched them shift and clench their hands and jaws almost in unison.

The Marshal knew these telltale warning signs all too well. He didn't want to frighten them any more than he had to, but he couldn't allow them to cultivate the notion of turning bloody. He considered his words carefully before speaking again. "I know what y'all are thinking, and you better stop thinking it, right now. I don't want to hurt no one, but, Son, you pull on me and I *will* show you what fast looks like." His voice was cold as a slab of granite.

"No, Sir, we don't want no trouble," Daniel said weakly, his eyes wide as the clear blue sky.

"That's good, Son. Neither do I. Y'all head on back with me, make your apologies, and take yer lumps and that'll be the end of it. Swear on my star, boys," he said.

"Danny, we can't trust him. We can't trust him, not if Judge Foster sent him," Jimmy Thomas blurted.

"Jimmy, I said I don't want to hurt y'all. None of y'all. I just want to get you home to your folks, and that's the truth." Jackson said it as quickly as he could, seeing that Jimmy's accusation had unnerved the other boys.

"My Pa says Judge Foster ain't no good, and y'all can't trust him none. He says the man's cruel and likes to hurt people," Jimmy said in a low voice.

The Marshal felt the situation had almost been defused, but Jimmy Thomas couldn't keep his mouth shut and now had Jackson fighting to find the right words. He knew he couldn't agree with Jimmy's statement, but on the other hand, he didn't want to defend Jimmy's accusation and indirectly call the boy's father a liar. Moment after silent moment passed as Jackson racked his mind and felt sweat form on his brow, fire catching in his ears. The lawman soon abandoned his search for words as he noticed all three boys had their gazes fixed upon the same point just over Jackson's right shoulder. Something, or someone, was behind the Marshal.

In one smooth motion, Jackson Bennett French wheeled and brought both barrels of his shotgun to bear. The Marshal finished cocking both hammers on his double-barrels, then stopped and felt as though a hot branding iron had been pressed onto his heart. Behind him was the tiny form of Daniel's younger brother Samuel, pointing a Cattleman's Revolver at Jackson's chest. The boy was nine years old.

For Jackson Bennett French, today would be that day.

...those who can claim innocence by their own hand shall be forever beyond the reach of the Reaper's scythe...

—Excerpt from the Book of Life

Mourning Dove Song

Part 2

It was early morning in the Marshal's office. Jackson Bennett French was finally about to enjoy his coffee after it finished brewing on the stovetop. These days, the sweet and bitter drink was a necessity to get the veteran lawman up and ready for the day. Jackson rose from his desk and took his tin cup with him to the stove at the far end of the room. He poured a tall cup of coffee from the pot and scooped a couple spoonfuls of sugar into the beverage. He tasted the drink; it was still a little too bitter for his liking. He instinctually reached for the sugar spoon but stopped himself short, remembering the loving yet judgmental voice of his wife Marry in his ear.

"You know that the doctor says you need to hold off on the sweets. They are not good for your heart," she would say each time she caught him trying to enjoy some confectionary delight. She was right, though. As time passed, his body had become more unforgiving of his diet. The Marshal had done everything he could to keep from having Marry let out his trousers an inch or two and he was not about to give her ammunition for her well-intentioned scolding. He knew she loved him dearly, as he did her, and that she just worried about his health as any Marshal's wife would do. They both knew this job took its toll on a family, and even more for a man later in his life.

Jackson spent a few more moments reflecting and sipped his coffee once again. Still, it was just too bitter for him. He could bear it no more; if he was going to drink it, he wanted to be able to enjoy it. The Marshal reached for the sugar spoon and lumped a third scoop of white crystals into his dark brown drink. He could hear Marry's chastising each time he put the cup to his lips but justified his behavior with the rationale that he would be retiring and hanging up his star at the end of the year. He figured that fact should buy a measure of good will from Marry, helping to maintain a state of marital bliss at home.

The past year had been the hardest year Jackson Bennett French had ever served as a Marshal. It had not been the same since that day. *That day*. Not a morning passed when he didn't think about what happened out on the prairie with those boys. *That day* had made Jackson want to leave the service. He had nearly thrown down his star and gun belt that very afternoon—but did not. Somehow, he'd managed to live with it, but he was not sure he could ever tell anyone what really happened out there—nor that he could ever forgive himself for what he had done.

To make matters worse, Jackson Bennett French had not had a warrant hit his desk since that day. In the past, when the Marshal had been haunted by a difficult case, he was able to realign his focus when duty called and he had to saddle up. Now, there was little to occupy his time more than drinking his morning coffee, walking the town and tipping his hat to those he passed, and cleaning and re-cleaning his forty-fives, just in case they somehow had gotten dirty while stowed in his gun belt. Even Annabel had started to grow restless, tied off outside the Marshal's station all day. This rest in lawlessness was something Jackson would have welcomed in younger years, but an old man had many memories to visit in the stillness.

Jackson wondered if this was what it would be like to retire. He admitted to himself that he'd never really thought of what would come next for him. He'd never been able to picture himself doing anything besides being a Marshal, but now that their son had grown and moved east, it would just be Jackson and Marry in their cottage. He didn't dread being alone with Marry for days on end; they loved each other dearly. Moreover, they both genuinely enjoyed each other's company. The challenge for the Marshal was in thinking how to fill the vast sprawls of time he would have on his hands outside of conversation over the kitchen table. The size of his savings ensured that he would not have to do anything to support his family in retirement, but he could not simply be a man of leisure. Jackson Bennett French needed to be a useful man. He didn't know how to relax.

Perhaps taking up farming or carpentry would be a way for him to stay busy in his twilight years. The Marshal admitted that either notion remained only a fantasy; while crops or woodwork might occupy his hands, nether would fulfill his spirit. Trades and agriculture were honorable enough pursuits, but Jackson needed something which spoke to the nature of right against wrong and order against chaos. He supposed that need had attracted him to the service of the law in the first place. Perhaps he would run for a judge's office. Several people had posed the notion to him over the years, and he knew he would be a good judge. But Marry would never stand for it. It would mean just as much time away from home as when he wore a tin star, if not more. He had not spent nearly enough nights lying beside his beloved wife as she deserved, and he had sworn he would be closer to home after he hung up his guns.

Perhaps they could pack up and move east to be near their

son Joseph while Jackson helped manage his bank. Marry would like the notion of being closer to their baby. That was a thought for sure, but it would mean living in a city. Both Jackson and Marry loved the range; the sun breaking over the open prairie was not something either one would want to sacrifice. Besides, a city was no place for Annabel, and Jackson would not do wrong by the other important lady in his life. He realized ranches and stables existed in the northeast, and they could see Joseph living near a city just as well as living in a city. Most importantly, moving east would mean Jackson would never have any of the physical reminders of some of his darker days as a Marshal. That would likely be enough to tip the scales. He and his wife had not had any formal discussion about what life would be like for them in Jackson's retirement, and he felt it might be a good opportunity to broach the subject with Marry and their son when Joseph came to visit at the end of the week.

For the first time since deciding to leave the service, the Marshal allowed himself to wonder what might become of the office and who would take over. He glanced at each of the three empty desks in the room belonging to his deputies. Mark and Paul were both much younger and had a lot still to learn, but they were each fine lawmen. Brandon had served with Jackson for twenty years now, and he was the logical choice for taking over the position. Brandon had the knowledge, judgment, and nerve for this business, but, truth be told, he was not far behind Jackson when it came to the small amount of time left in the service. Brandon had been talking about packing it in for nearly half the number of years he'd ridden with Jackson.

Several other Marshal stations in the adjacent territories had men well-fitted to the role in terms of experience. Jackson's concern with having a Marshal reassigned to take his place was the fact that his successor would be a stranger to the town. He felt it important for the people who resided within a Marshal's jurisdiction to be familiar with that Marshal. The Marshals were responsible for protecting the families of their neighbors, after all.

Jackson reached into his waistcoat and pulled out his pocket watch to check the hour. It was now past midday and he started to wonder where his deputies had gone. He'd sent them to accompany a prisoner exchange while they handed over a man to their southern office, but they should have been back by now, unless they stopped to take lunch on their return. They would have passed through the town of River Fork, which had a little cantina there with some of the best corn chili Jackson had ever eaten. He could understand if his deputies wanted a slight delay so they could fill their bellies. It was still early for alarm, but Jackson had always been the cautious type with a propensity to fear the worst.

Normally, he would have ridden with his men, but he felt it necessary for them to get a sense of how things were done without him. All three of his deputies took direction very well, but a Marshal needed to be able to think on his feet and trust his own instinct. Jackson had struggled with the decision to remain behind on this job, not because he wanted to do something beyond watching the sun in the sky through the station windows, but because the man they were transferring was a personal acquaintance—and one of the cruelest fugitives Jackson had ever run down.

Sari Tapper was the worst Jackson Bennett French had ever seen. The man had no limits. Arson, robbery, murder, kidnapping—the man had done it all and more. He was the most dangerous kind of outlaw, because more than money or infamy, Sari just liked to hurt people, to cause pain. As a Marshal, Jackson had spent close to ten years hunting Sari before he finally put him in chains, but the Marshal never could understand the man's sadistic lust. Jackson believed it was most likely due to the fact that Sari was half-tribal. His father was a small-time criminal, who managed to drink himself to death when Sari was just a boy, and his mother was a full-blooded tribal, as wild as they came. Her people had shunned her for her bastard child, and the woman had taken work as a whore.

Jackson had very few occasions to meet tribal folk face to face, as they mostly kept to their own kind out on the plains. The stories he'd heard of the tribals' way of life were haunting, even if only a handful of those tales held truth. Some said they drank the blood of the dead. Others said they would cut their own bodies as a sign of pride and spiritual devotion. Some said the tribal ancestors of long ago lived in the land far to the south, where the prairie turned into tropical jungle, and they worshipped the giant cracks in the earth there which spewed molten slag and fire into the sky as some kind of living deity. He had even once heard a story that when it came time for a tribal elder to die, they would set themselves on fire. While Jackson had barely ever had run-ins with tribals outside of Sari Tapper, he always got the sense from those he did meet of a deep, underlying rage burning in the belly of their people.

Being half-tribal meant Sari remained both trapped between two worlds and an outsider in each. The full-blooded tribals looked at him as tainted, with impure blood, while everyone else only saw him as a savage's child. The mixing of a tribal and an outlaw had been like trying to put out a fire with dynamite. The only world Sari knew was the one which had taught him hatred, and he'd learned that lesson well. The man had been a survivor from day one; with the deck stacked against him, Sari Tapper was forced to become sharp and quick-witted.

Jackson knew a great deal of luck had been with him the day he'd finally brought in the outlaw. But he would take it as he could get it. What mattered to the lawman was that Sari was in a cage now and wouldn't be able to harm any more innocents.

He was called back to the present when a delicate figure darkened the doorway to the Marshal's station—his darling Marry. She stood there, silhouetted in the sunlight shining through the open doorway, as beautiful as the first day the Marshal laid eyes on her. Time seemed to have no effect on this woman; she was still perfect.

"Good afternoon, Marshal French," Marry said with a soft voice and wide smile.

"Good afternoon, Mrs. French." Jackson stood and tipped his hat to his wife.

"I made some beef stew and figured it was about time for you to take lunch. So I wanted to bring you something warm to eat," Marry said. She nodded to the towel-covered basket she carried in the crook of her arm. "You haven't eaten yet, have you? Did you have any designs on lunch?"

"No, ma'am, I have not," Jackson said, and realized he was actually very hungry. Almost on queue, the Marshal's stomach let out a low rumble.

"Jackson, I swear, sometimes you would forget to breathe," his wife scolded with a tiny shake of her head.

"I do forget to breathe sometimes. I'm just lucky I have you to remind me." Jackson's smile showed through his thick silver mustache.

His wife stepped inside the Marshal's station and made her way to Jackson's desk, where she put down her basket before greeting her husband with a hug and a kiss. They sat at his desk and Marry withdrew a couple of small, cast-iron crocks from the basket and a pair of matching place settings. She uncovered the two crocks and the room instantly filled with the rich, savory aroma of the beef stew. Husband and wife ate a loving meal together, talking of the little things. Marry always helped to remind him that things still happened in the world beyond the tin star.

"What's the occasion?" Jackson asked. "Not that I'm complaining to a home-cooked meal with my gal, mind you, but you don't normally see me at the station unless there's something going on."

"A letter from Joseph came in the post today. He says he has big news he wants to share with us on his visit." Marry smiled.

"What news is that?"

"I just said he wants to tell us when he gets in." She rolled her eyes a little. "I swear, sometimes it's like talking to a horse."

"Thank you, love. Annabel is a fine listener," Jackson said playfully. "You think it's that Jenny girl he's been writing us about?"

"Goodness, I hope so. It's far past time for our boy to have settled down. He's done us so proud and he deserves a good woman." Marry sighed.

"Truer words," the Marshal said with a nod. "You know, there's some news of my own that I've been thinking over today, and I wanted to bring it up while Joseph was here. But now I think might be a better time to talk it over together," Jackson said.

"Why, Jackson Bennett French, I must say you have my attention. Before you start talking, I have a little something of my own for you." Marry reached into the basket again to withdraw and unwrap a bundled pie plate, revealing a still hot and steaming, freshly baked apple pie.

"Ma'am, I hope you know that trying to bribe a Marshal is a crime," Jackson said with eyes wide and mouth watering.

"Our boy's letter put me in such a good mood, I had to bring your favorite to mark the day," Marry said.

Screams of alarm broke the intimate moment between them. Faster than the eye could follow, the Marshal was on his feet with guns drawn, standing between the station door and his wife. The tension of danger grew even more when Jackson made sense of the jumbled sounds ringing outside, and he heard his name called above the commotion. He placed the voice of his deputy, Paul. The sound of hooves coming to a halt, followed by boots on wood, signaled Paul's arrival before the deputy appeared at the door.

Paul stumbled into the station a bloody mess. Jackson holstered his guns and immediately went to support his weakened deputy. "Marry! Go on and fetch doc Robin," he called, bracing Paul and leading him to sit on the cot in the station's holding cell.

"Oh, Paul," Marry gasped, then quickly left the station to

retrieve the town doctor.

Paul sat on the cot in the holding cell, clutching his forearm and trying to stop the flow of blood trickling from the bullet wound. Jackson looked in horror at what had been done to the young man. Paul's left ear was cut clean off his skull, leaving only torn flesh and caked blood in its place. The man's left eye had been put out as well; the deputy kept his eyelid shut over the empty hole as best he could but had difficulty managing it amidst the plethora of cuts and bruises littering his face.

"It was Sari," Paul said through blood-soaked teeth.

"That's plain enough to see. Don't you speak. The doc is coming," Jackson said as reassuringly as he could.

"No, I can talk just fine. It's what he wanted me to do. He wanted me to give you a message, so he only took one ear and one eye. He didn't trust me to make it back full blind and deaf." Paul cringed with a renewed shock of pain.

"Damn that man!" Jackson snarled.

"Sari somehow had a posse hit us before we met up with the southern office boys. Must have been seven or eight of 'em. I went down first and didn't come back up 'til the shooting had stopped." Paul raised his forearm to indicate his battle wound. "Sari wanted me to tell you that he don't want to run again. He just wants you to meet him."

"Damn right I'll meet him! I'll have every Marshal in the territory hunt him down!" Jackson spat.

"No. He said he won't have it like that. He just wants you alone. He said he would wait for you at the mile marker outside Watertown come the end of the week. He said if you come alone, he won't run, but if he sees a posse after him, he'll make you chase him to the ends of the prairie and he'll burn everything in his path." The deputy fought to get the words out through the sting of his wounds.

There were a few moments of silence between the Marshal and his deputy. "Brandon and Mark?" Jackson asked, knowing the answer already. Paul shook his head and reached into his waistcoat pocket to withdraw two tin stars. Jackson took them and fought to keep from breaking.

"It were quick for both of 'em. They went on their feet, and Sari never had a chance to work on 'em like he did me," Paul said.

"Small mercy, that."

"Jackson Bennett French, you will *not* do what you're thinking of doing," came Marry's voice from the station doorway. The Marshal and his deputy turned to look at her; she had the slight and even frail-looking doctor Robin in tow.

Jackson stood and went to his wife. "It's not personal. I would let someone else take this one, but if I go alone, that could spare a lot of lives. I don't want to take the chance of turning Sari Tapper loose on the territory again," the Marshall stated.

"It's sure enough a trick. You can't believe Sari Tapper will do as he says," Marry pleaded.

"In all the time I spent chasing the man, I never made him for a liar. He may be a lot of vile things," Jackson said, "but when he says he'll do something, he keeps to his word."

"Why can't you let this one rest?" Marry asked. There was a thick silence, and Jackson was slow to respond.

"Because I've given a lot of good lawmen's widows a lot of tin stars folded in a lot of territory flags in my time. Now I have to go and give two new widows two more tin stars folded in territory flags. And I'm sayin' no more before I'm done." Jackson nodded stiffly and frowned down at her.

"What about you? What about your star?" Marry spoke softly.

"Like I said, no more. Nothing is going to stop me from coming home to you, Marry. Not Sari Tapper, not nothing."

...And I alone shall visit the tomb of the King Who Shall Never Reign. For all others, this will be a forbidden place...

—Excerpt from the Personal Writings of the Fourth Horseman

Mourning Dove Song

Part 3

This would be his last day wearing a star. One way or another, Jackson Bennett French would no longer serve as a Marshal after today. It was the deal he'd had to strike with his darling Marry—were he to pursue the fugitive Sari Tapper, it would be his last duty as a Marshal.

Jackson had planned to retire in less than a year, but the recent events after Sari's escape from custody had caused him to rethink his decision to step away. His retirement would have seen his office reduced from one Marshal and three deputies to one Marshal and two deputies. That would have been plenty of good men to handle the kind of law needed in the territory until a third deputy could be assigned. But after Sari Tapper had slain two of Jackson's men, it meant that the Marshal's office would be reduced to a single man should he retire. Added to that, the fact that his last deputy Paul was missing an eye and an ear gave the Marshal a considerable amount of pain and worry to think about laying down his star. What kind of lawman would he be if he left his people with only one man between them and those who would do them harm?

That was when Marry had stepped in. For too long, she'd let her husband be the one who folks leaned on to make order out of anarchy. Perhaps Marry's greatest mercy lay in telling her husband when enough had been enough. Jackson knew that, without her voice of reason in his ear, he would let the tin star drive him to the grave. It still took some mighty convincing, and even a little threatening on his wife's part, but in the end, Marry had yet again broken through to Jackson's sensibilities.

No man would question the decades of distinguished service the Marshal had offered, and if he said it was time to retire and they needed to find men to fill his boots, that was what would happen. Anyone who said otherwise would have to answer to the Marshal's wife. Marry did understand, though, that her husband needed this final track as much as she needed him to retire. Jackson had to finish Sari Tapper once and for all. He needed to see the man's cruelty put to an end from which there would be no return.

The break of the sun on the prairie was without words to describe its majesty, the figure of the Marshal atop his mount the only shape on the horizon. He felt, on these long rides, that somehow the rest of the world ceased to move and nothing existed beyond him and the animal carrying him. Jackson raced the dawn as he always did when on the trail of a fugitive. The Marshal and Annabel had been up before the sun and on the move when the sky turned from muted shades of grey to rich tones of vibrant blue, white, and gold.

Watertown was fast approaching, the markers passing them by one after another. The five-mile marker had just been buried in a cloud of Annabel's dust as the Marshal and his horse thundered down the trail toward the place Sari Tapper had said he would wait for the man. The next wooden stake on the path would be the one-mile marker to Watertown.

Jackson Bennett French wondered if Sari Tapper would be alone or if the fugitive would have his gang with him. Paul had said it seven or eight men had sprang Sari out of his bonds. Jackson had faced odds like that before and survived, but only barely and when he was a much younger man. The Marshal knew this could likely be a trap, but he had to take the chance, however small. Jackson Bennett French could not live with himself and the knowledge that he willfully unleashed Sari Tapper on the territory once again.

He'd noted the terms of Sari Tapper's message through Paul. The outlaw claimed he would stand fast if the Marshal came alone, but he made no mention of any condition to come alone himself. Jackson had mentally prepared himself to face as many as ten hardened criminals that morning. He also took physical measures to ensure that, if he were to be ended by overwhelming odds today, it would not be for a lack of shooting back. Jackson had stowed a lever-action and his double-barrel in Annabel's saddle bags. He had his gun belt fully loaded and had added an extra pair of holstered long-barrel forty-fives.

The Marshal did feel some ease with the likelihood that the coming confrontation would actually be two men meeting alone. He knew if someone wanted to ambush a man, the best place to do so was anywhere other than where the intended target planned to go. Jackson had seen no sign of Sari's men on the road, and it would be only minutes before the Marshal reached the appointed place.

Even if there was no dirty dealing on Sari's behalf when it came to numbers, Jackson was sure the half-blood meant to kill him. He knew his man better than anyone else, and Sari was a killer, plain and simple. It was what he did—cold and heartless. Sari had a great flair for revenge; he once slipped a rattlesnake between the bedsheets of a man who had cheated him at a game of Hold 'em. He'd collapsed a mine shaft on one of his men he only suspected of trying to leave his gang. The list of tales of retribution ran wider than the river cutting through Valley Canyon when it came to Sari Tapper.

The Marshal feared to reckon what the half-blood had in store for the man who had forced Sari to spend near half his life in chains and behind bars.

The Marshal saw an outline of a man across the prairie sprawling before him. It looked like Sari Tapper had kept to his word, as Jackson had expected. He came up on the mile marker to Watertown—and the shape beside it. It seemed, suddenly, that Sari Tapper had not waited for Jackson alone; the Marshal spotted three other riders with the half-blood. Jackson wondered where the remaining men in Sari's gang may have been. Perhaps they'd concealed themselves somewhere, but then the flats of the prairie offered minimal opportunities for a man to hide, let alone four or five men with horses. Maybe the rest of the outlaw's men had parted ways after springing the man from the prison transfer.

Jackson had to admit that Sari's plan to wait for a Marshal to come find him, and trust that he would come without a full posse, would likely not appeal to most outlaws. Maybe Paul had just gotten the count wrong and there had only been three other men all along. The deputy would not have been the first man to misrepresent how many were on the other side of a shootout. Sometimes it was for pride's sake, or maybe Paul's injuries caused him to lose focus of the battle and forget the details.

However it had played out, Jackson Bennett French only knew that he now looked at four armed criminals. He felt a calm take hold when he realized he'd brought more than one gun for each man he might have to draw down. The Marshal slowed his mount to a trot; he didn't want to spook the men by coming up on them too fast. If the outlaw wanted to talk, Jackson would let him talk. He doubted, however, that this encounter would actually end with only words exchanged. Jackson pushed the folds of his long brown coat behind the grips of the forty-fives at his hips so he could draw them quickly when the time arrived. He wanted to be prepared for whatever came next.

Up close, Jackson could better see who they were. The two to Sari's left were strangers to the Marshal, but they both sported matching red bandanas tied around their necks and had brown eyes and similar features. The pair were younger men and looked close in age. Jackson guessed they were brothers, or at least related in some way. Likely, the duo were aspiring outlaws looking to make a name by riding with the notorious Sari Tapper. Most importantly, Jackson noted that each man only sported a single revolver on their hip as weapons, and the position of their guns implied they were both lefties. *Interesting family trait there*, Jackson thought.

On Sari Tapper's right stood a much older man. Jackson could not be sure, but he would wager with confidence that the man was Garret Hard, the last remaining member of Sari's original gang who hadn't been accounted for when Jackson had made the captures. The man looked to be the right age, but it wasn't as easy for Jackson to tell if the wild white hair had actually once before been the blonde, curly locks of the Garret Hard he'd met so many years before. The greatest indicator, though, was the sawed-off single-barrel shotgun resting in the crook of the man's arms. It was a fairly uncommon choice of weapon, and Garret Hard was one very few men Jackson had ever encountered who favored such a firearm. Garret had served as Sari Tapper's second in command for the later years during which the half-blood rode the plains. It would stand to reason that, if anyone had the gumption to go in on a jail break for Sari Tapper two decades after he had been put away, it would have been Garret Hard.

There was Sari Tapper in the middle. The years in prison had taken a heavy toll on the outlaw. His face sported more scars than fair skin, and the flesh which remained unmarred looked hard as leather. Jackson wondered how many of the scars gracing Sari's face had been the result of a fellow prisoner or guard and how many had been made by the man's own hand. The tribals had some perverse predisposition to cut their own skin, something about it making them stronger or that it showed devotion to their faith. That was how the tales were told, anyway. Jackson figured Sari just wanted to see blood, and in the absence of an innocent victim, the outlaw had made do with his own hide. The half-blood had a forty-five holstered on each hip.

The Marshal gave pause for a moment. He did not know how this next scene would play out. His hands were ready to find the grip on his guns in a split second, and the lawman watched the quartet of criminals with an unblinking eye. Sari Tapper moved first. The half-blood did not go to guns but instead slowly and gently dismounted his horse. The three other riders followed suit and stood on the flat of the prairie.

Jackson gave it a breath before he stepped down from his seat on Annabel's back, and the outlaws slowly approached the Marshal. "That's close enough, Tapper," Jackson called once they had come within fifteen paces. The four men stopped, and nothing disturbed them but the wind blowing across the wide open range between them.

Then, everything was dead still for a few heartbeats. In that time, Jackson felt his brow moisten and his ears fills with fire. Those sensations always overcame him whenever he stood down a fugitive. Funny how the same thing happened whenever Marry caught him with his hand in the crock before dinner was served, though it was far easier for the Marshal to steady his nerves against an entire gang of armed men than it was to endure the scolding of his wife. It amused him even more that the image of that woman's gentle disappointment served as the tool he used to steel himself before a foreseeably violent situation.

"I see you came alone like I told you to. That was foolish," Sari Tapper said with a smile, showing his remaining yellow-and-brown-stained teeth.

Jackson knew how this would go. His hands readied to draw. "I knew you would run if you saw a posse coming," the Marshal said.

"I wanted to be sure I'd get close to you, and I know you'd never pass up a chance to get the man who got you first. Thing is, I took you down once on my own, and I'll do it again."

"You're an even bigger fool if you thought I was ever going to run. I got the lung rot and won't likely see past the winter. This is just about getting something back from the man who locked me in a hole for twenty years before I go cold," Sari said as his lips flung large globs of spittle and phlegm.

"Well, here I am," Jackson said with deadly purpose. The Marshal felt the touch of fire in his trigger fingers. He knew what came next.

"Yes, here you are."

The brother in the red bandana on the far left drew first. Jackson saw it and let his hands fall to his guns. That same man fired first, followed by a shot from his brother. One round hit the dust at the Marshal's boots and the other whizzed over his head. Both young men were quick in the hands but had not bothered to aim properly.

Jackson remained calm and cocked the hammer of his left-side long-barrel forty-five as he cleared his holster. He knelt, making himself a smaller target, and took careful aim to send three rounds of hot lead screaming through the air. The first hit the leftmost man square in the chest and dropped him to the ground. The second round struck his brother in the arm, but the third of the Marshal's shots landed squarely between the man's eyes and sent him to the dirt beside his brother.

Jackson felt a load of buckshot whip past his shoulder and cheek, tearing through the outermost sleeve of his coat on the right side but missing the flesh of his arm. Jackson wheeled his aim and fired the three remaining shots from his left side. The motion and the shotgun blast which had nearly hit him caused the lawman's aim to waiver, and the first two shots missed Garret Hard. But the third struck him in the left leg and brought him to one knee. Jackson dropped the gun in his left hand and smoothly drew the gun on his right.

Several shots from Sari Tapper's duel revolvers blazed past the Marshal. The half-blood fired wildly, launching shot after shot without minding his target. Jackson had the forty-five in his right hand cocked as he drew it and fired once quickly from his hip. The shot struck Sari Tapper low in his gut. Jackson let his left hand fan the hammer of his gun, rapidly sending the five remaining bullets sailing toward the two wounded outlaws.

After the Marshal had emptied his second gun, Garret Hard lay dead and Sari Tapper remained on his knees, trying to staunch the flow of blood from three bullet holes riddling his body. Jackson gave it a second to make sure the other men would not rise again, then drew one of the guns slung on his back. The Marshal approached Sari as the outlaw bled out in the dust beneath.

"You're the biggest fool. You don't even know I beat you." Sari Tapper laughed through a series of bloody coughs.

"It's over. Yer done," said Jackson.

"No. Before it's over, you will die, and there'll be screaming and blood." Sari Tapper laughed wildly like a mad man. One final shot from the Marshal silenced him forever.

That was it. With one final pull of the trigger Jackson Bennett French had done his final service as a Marshal of the Western Territories. He looked about at the dead and broken bodies of the men in the dust before him and realized he would never have to endure this sight again. The notion lifted his sprit. Jackson could be free of a vocation which walked hand-in-hand with death and suffering.

He returned calmly to Annabel and saddled up. "Come on, girl," he said to his loyal mount, and the two headed home.

He thought of how nice it would be to return to his wife and son, able to assure them he would never again be called to put himself in harm's way for the sake of his profession. The sun set as Jackson and Annabel made the final strides toward their homestead. He relished the chance to enjoy a warm meal at the table with his family, not having to worry about rising early in the morning. Then he caught the scent of smoke on the wind.

His body went cold the instant he saw the black plumes of smoke cast against the setting sun on the horizon. Jackson's home was burning.

Spurring Annabel on hard, he pushed fantasies of the worst imagining from his mind in the agonizing stretch of road between him and his home. His fears became realized, though, when he finally came upon his house and found it engulfed in flames. In one singular, earth-shattering moment, Jackson's previous nightmarish doubts became childish fears in comparison to the reality before him. Two figures hung from the desert willow growing in the front yard.

He stopped Annabel short of the tree and the mortifying display adorning its branches. When he had awoken that morning, he had been a husband and father. Now, unbelievably, Jackson Bennett French was a widower and childless. He pulled the bodies of his wife and son from the tree and held them in his arms. Covered in the blood of his family, the Marshal wept; he screamed into the smoky sky, and above all, he cursed the name of Sari Tapper.

His whole life had been destroyed. He could not bear the sight of the only beautiful things he had known in this world set to flame. Jackson mounted Annabel once more and rode, pressing his horse harder and harder as if, were he to get far enough from the tragic scene, it somehow would be undone. He dug his spurs into Annabel's heaving flanks, forcing her to gallop faster than she ever had before. He swore that if she moved any faster, she might yet take flight into the heavens above the prairie.

Jackson and Annabel rode long and far into the setting sun, traveling without direction save away—away from what lay behind.

Not long after the last bit of golden sunlight disappeared, Annabel fell. She could carry Jackson no longer; he'd ridden her to her breaking point. The grey mare would never carry a rider again in this life. The two were left cold and isolated on the prairie as dusk turned to night, and then into day again. And again...and again.

Then, in the darkest hour, in the dead of night, on the prairie without water, warmth, or hope, in a desolate place filled with nothing but cold—cold beyond cold—the Reaper came to collect the Marshal. Jackson Bennett French was far from free of a vocation filled with death and suffering. He had further still to ride.

...The river Praytos flows through the whole of the Fourth Horseman's Kingdom. At river's end is a burned willow tree, sprouted from tears of anguish and pain. Beneath its twisted branches is a well, fed by the river of spirits. From this well, life is made anew. And so shall it begin again in changed form...

—Excerpt from the Book of Life

Broken Steel, Broken Words

Part 1

A man trapped between duty and conscience is a tortured spirit indeed.

Sir Lionel James had come to know that plight well. There had never been a full marriage of the prized ideal of knighthood he'd sought in his youth and the reality of knighthood he came to know in his service to King Olok. Most of all, over the past few years, the objections of the knight's heart had become increasingly more commonplace as he faithfully executed his king's orders.

Sir Lionel knew that King Olok had to make nearly impossible decisions every day and that the king's doubters could not comprehend the weight of the crown. Even still, the knight felt himself questioning both his own devotion to his duty and his station as Captain of the Royal Guard. It seemed as though King Olok was a different man of late, or perhaps Sir Lionel saw His Royal Highness from a new perspective. It unsettled the knight to think that perhaps he fought for the wrong side, but each time he felt such creeping suspicions take hold within his heart, he forced himself to quash them. Sir Lionel steadied his resolve when it waivered by telling himself he was unaware of all the facts and that the path he walked had been forged by men older and wiser than himself.

Sir Lionel turned his focus outward and reflected on his immediate duty. He had been charged to parley with Sir Gunn to express the desires of the king. Sir Lionel held a deep respect for Sir Gunn, a man who had served a highly distinguished term for King Olok. Some even said the king had taken Sir Gunn on as a sort of protégé for a time. Now, Sir Gunn and King Olok had experienced a parting of ways.

Sir Lionel was not privy to the root cause of the rift, but he knew the king and Sir Gunn had not spoken in person for nearly a year now, and that Sir Gunn had left the royal court to hold himself up within the confines of his personal estate even longer than that. He hoped Sir Gunn would listen to reason. The Captain of the Guard did not wish to dwell on the required course of action should he fail in returning King Olok and Sir Gunn to amicable terms.

He hated this great sense of division brewing within the kingdom. Never had the knight dreamed that the disquiet in the outer reaches of the realm would spread so fast or so far. Sir Lionel certainly never thought he would ever see the Knighthood stand divided. Ever since he was a boy, the kingdom had known its share of war, famine, plague, and veritable trials, but this tension and civil unrest among the king's subjects remained a new and looming danger. These were trying and unknown times, to be sure.

Sir Lionel lifted his eyes from the dusty wooden floor of Sir Gunn's dining hall as he heard the sounds of approaching footsteps and clinking armor. He stood when Sir Gunn entered the room and offered a friendly smile which the other knight returned. The men then met, sharing a warrior's grip and a brotherly embrace.

"I thank you for receiving me at this late hour, Sir Gunn. Your hospitality is most generous," Sir Lionel said with a widening smile.

"I will always open my home to you, Sir Lionel. Honorable men are welcome here." Sir Gunn took a seat at the head of his long table.

The fireplace had long cooled and only a few scattered and flickering candles remained as the source of light in the room. It looked as though Sir Gunn's estate had recently declined into disrepair. Sir Lionel had noticed only a handful of servants as he traversed the grounds, and that number of able-bodied attendants was suited only for a household perhaps a tenth the size. Sir Lionel wondered whether or not the reduction in staff was a matter of financial necessity. King Olok had recently commanded the second increase in quarterly duties this year, and nobility and commoner alike had felt the squeeze of the crown's purse strings. The king's taxes were, in part, the reason for Sir Lionel's dispatch here to Sir Gunn's home.

"It is good to see you, my friend. It has been a long time since last we met. I am ashamed to say that I cannot fully recall our last encounter," Sir Lionel stated.

"There is no call for shame, brother. I do not so easily remember all the events of my final days at the royal court." Sir Gunn paused as he seemed to recount some haunting past story. "That was a complicated time." His voice trailed off before he returned to the present. "The thing which matters most is that you are here, now." The man forced a half smile.

"Agreed," said Sir Lionel. His felt an undisguisable frown weigh his brow as he knew he must speak of the king's wishes with his knightly brother. "I wish this truly was a social matter," he said, "but I am here as an official of the crown."

"I understand," Sir Gunn said. "Knights of the crown are never truly free of duty, much less the Captain of the King's Guard. I respect the directness of your motives." He folded his hands in front of him and made ready to hear his guest's words.

"His Royal Highness King Olok bade me speak with you and

make his wishes known. I am here to speak to you as a fellow knight who has sworn an oath of service to the crown," Sir Lionel said. The words were clearly not easy to pass from his lips. He'd never been at ease speaking in another's stead, even the king's. There was silence for a moment as he tried to think of the most diplomatic way to phrase things.

"And what of the king's wishes? What does he command of this simple knight?" Sir Gunn asked. He was pushing Lionel on but refrained from letting his voice sound too coy.

"Understand that this is my duty to speak with you tonight. I must—we must do as we are commanded by His Royal Highness..." The frustrated conflict between his duty and his friendship appeared quite obvious in his speech.

Sir Gunn quickly interjected. "Brother, just speak. I know your honor is great and your sense of duty beyond question. You need not fear offense for merely repeating words commanded of you to be spoken." The knight shared his words calmly and gently, and they helped to ease his guest.

"King Olok commands you to return to the royal court." The words came out slowly and seemed harder to think than to finally say.

"Is that all?" Sir Gunn asked with a raised eyebrow. "I do not think the king would send the Captain of the Royal Guard because he takes issue with where I choose to sleep at night." The corner of his mouth curled in a grin.

Sir Lionel felt the slightest chuckle desperate to escape but held it back. "No. That is not all." He was grateful for the levity Sir Gunn brought into the conversation, but it made the king's words no easier to speak. "The king also demands that you reaffirm your love and devotion to him...publicly. He requires you to remit your last two quarterly duties to the treasury...with an additional one tenth tithe for tardiness." He almost choked on the last words and set his lips together again in a grim line. The expression on Sir Gunn's face told him the man remained unsurprised by what he'd heard.

"Is that the whole of it?" he asked blankly, then sat back in his chair and crossed his arms over his chest.

"Yes, those are the wishes of the king in completion," Sir Lionel said.

"So, there it is, like always." Sir Gunn's voice was little more than a whisper. "Coin and vanity," he continued. The room had become like a grave—cold and silent.

"These are little things, are they not, Sir Gunn?"

"They may seem that way, but I fear the matter at hand is not as little as the request, simple though it may be," Sir Gunn said, his voice a distant measure of distain.

"So then, you will surrender to the requests of His Highness?" Lionel was confused by his host's aloof responses.

"Brother, I cannot do as the king asks," Sir Gunn said.

"I don't understand. If the matter separating you and the king is a simple thing, why can it not be reconciled?" He tried to keep the desperation from infecting his words and had to think carefully when choosing the next. "The increased duties are a strain for all the king's subjects. I do not wish to assume, but if it is a matter of the debt to the crown, the obstacle is far from insurmountable." Sir Lionel despised talk of money and did not wish to embarrass his friend, or himself. But he had to say it anyways. "I would pay the required fees with my own purse, if that would settle the matter."

"Thank you, brother. I appreciate your chivalry, but it is not a matter of the debt. At least, the debt is not the heart of the matter dividing the king and myself." It looked as though Sir Gunn wrestled himself with his own choice of words.

"Then please enlighten me. What is at the center of this feud? I swear I will do all within my power to make peace," Sir Lionel said.

"Be careful with the promises you make, especially when you swear so blindly," Sir Gunn said, locking eyes with his fellow know. "You may come to regret those words, brother. Do you still wish to know the cause of my objections?"

"I do."

"I cannot serve the crown in good conscience any longer, because the man who wears it is not fit to rule," Sir Gunn said. There was a tense moment of silence as the shock of his words settled into the room.

Finally, Sir Lionel gathered his wits and his breath. "Sir Gunn, think of what you are saying. Such an accusation can pass for treason."

"Brother, search your own conscience. You know in your heart of hearts that what I say is sound. Olok has been lost in his ways for a very long time." The man's face set in somber regret.

"I beg you, no more of this. King Olok will see your neck on the block for such disloyalty," Lionel pleaded. There was another long, painful silence, finally broken by Sir Gunn's heavy sigh.

"You have always known, haven't you? You were never good at masking your feelings, and I always saw it in your face. You rarely smiled or felt the pride of wearing the king's star like the rest of the Knight's Circle." Sir Gunn gestured to the black, eight-pointed star embroidered on the white tabard both knights wore over their chainmail.

The Blackstar on the cloth over his heart called Sir's Lionel's fingers to touch them, and he quickly took a moment to recount each of the eight knightly virtues represented by each of the Blackstar's points.

"Sir Gunn, I know it is not always easy to see the best of the star's points in every action. Their purposes often conflict with each other, and finding the balance can prove a challenge." He felt his heart sink when he recognized that his words were simply repeated doctrine, learned by each knight as a first-year initiate.

"For ten years, for ten *wretched* years, we marched on Olok's orders and lay siege to the mountains in the north. How many of our brothers died in the mud and snow of those mountains? And for what? Never once did Olok make his mind known for committing us to a campaign of war and blood. He alone knows the reason for ten long winters of butchery, if there is a reason," Sir Gunn said, shaking his head with utter disgust and disbelief. "Can you in good conscience tell me there was some subtle hint of virtue in ten years of death?"

"There must have been. I have to believe there we fought for something right in that war, even if I do not fully understand it. On some level, it must have been about protecting king and country. There is virtue in that, at least," Sir Lionel said with little more than a whisper. "This is what I tell myself to make sense of those winters spent in the mountains."

The two knights were silent for several moments after that. They each reflected on the king's knights who had given their lives for that war, as well as the men's lives they'd claimed on the battlefield. Both Sir Lionel and Sir Gunn quietly wondered what had been the purpose of all of it.

Sir Gunn's eyes reflected the preemptive self-wounding of his next words. "You know the most telling way I see your conscience at war with your sense of duty? You never willingly called me or any of the king's knights *Brother*," he said, slightly choking on the last word as he forced his eyes to remain dry. "You know we are family in title only, and the love we feel for one another is born of duty to the crown. It is not genuine passion and devotion. You have always known this. You have always felt that the Blackstar was a fantasy. We would claim virtue and still do as we pleased. You knew this even before you first wore the star. I only just came to accept this as truth, and that is why I can no longer serve Olok. But you have always known." The man visibly fought tears, now.

Sir Lionel tried to cling to his sense of duty, but he could only hear the truth screaming in his head, and it deafened him. "I rarely ever saw the king live up to the legend who preceded him. His actions these days are so far removed from the stories of the noble champion I heard spoken of him. I hold out hope that, perhaps one day, he will be the king I have longed to serve." Sir Lionel struggled with his own words, as part of him desperately wanted to give in to the king's critics and condemn the man as a fraud.

"I know the king's honor is not so easily seen," he continued, "but I cling to this belief. He may have created the star, but the eight virtues it represents transcend any living man. Their rightness is beyond question." He suddenly realized that, even as he spoke, he feared his own words. Feared himself. But he could not stop. "Perhaps the Blackstar is a fantasy, but I will never stop striving to bring the eight points to the world, to make them a reality. Not while I live. King or no king, this is what I will do."

"You were always one of the greatest among us," Sir Gunn said. "Men follow you. They would fight for you and they would die for you. I would. It wrenches my gut to see the king command better men than himself."

"Then please, I beg of you, come back. If not for Olok, then for me and the eight points."

"I'm sorry, brother, but the die is cast. I cannot. I share your belief in our ways and I admire your belief in the king. But I myself do not hold the same faith in Olok. I am certain of this," Sir Gunn stated. His face softened in an expression of acceptance before he continued. "I know what is about to happen, and I want you to know I am at peace with it."

"Please, Sir Gunn," Lionel begged.

"No. I ask you to return to the king and tell him I will not do as he commands." Sir Gunn stood from the table. "I love you, brother. Goodbye." This time the man did nothing to hide his tears.

Sir Lionel rose to meet the other knight and embraced the man. "I love you too, brother." He departed quickly from the estate while he still had his wits about him.

He had just passed the final bend to put the far gate of Sir Gunn's home out of view when he lay eyes on the two armed infantry detachments waiting for his return.

The sergeant major stepped forward and addressed him. "You are alone, sir. Then Sir Gunn's treason is assured?" the soldier asked.

"He will not return to the king. Make of that what you will. I'll not stay for what is next." He made every attempt to conceal the rage he felt inside.

He spurred his mount on as the sergeant major ordered the men to advance on Sir Gunn's estate with weapons drawn and shields fronted. As Sir Lionel listened to the marching of armored soldiers fade in the distance, his hand touched the Blackstar on his breast once more. *Eight knightly virtues: Honor, Loyalty, Chivalry, Commitment, Truth, Justice, Faith, and Tenacity,* he thought. *A good man will be killed tonight, and I will not stop it. Where is the virtue in that?*

"I have reigned over Purgatory for longer than any dynasty in the realm of man. I have reigned longer than any ten dynasties, and my kingdom has seen the fall of countless empires in the realm above. The prospect of eternity is not unknown to me. I knew its meaning well in the time of the Unity, though I would not care to spend the endless march of time in this world of darkness and cold, simply waiting for one moment to fade into the next. I am Lord Master here, and as such, I will not share in the torment of those condemned to my kingdom. More so, I am thought to be wicked, cruel, and wholly without compassion, and I will see these accusations ruled as slander. I will defeat the onslaught of nothingness with the promise of epic spectacle and prove my benevolence to all in grand fashion. So I decree, that once a generation, on the sixty-sixth day of the sixty-sixth year, Purgatory shall host a great tournament. Its contestants shall be chosen from among the finest warriors damned to the currents of the Praytos. My court shall revel in gruesome display as the chosen spirits battle each other into oblivion. In the end, when all but a single warrior has been vanquished, that final spirit shall reap the spoils of victory. I, Lord Master of Purgatory, shall be merciful and gracious, granting them life again and releasing them from Purgatory. So I command, and so shall it be done."

—Lord Master of Purgatory and Fourth Horseman, Death

Broken Steel, Broken Words

Part 2

King Olok's castle lay under siege. His people could take no more of his hypocrisy and had risen up in open rebellion against his reign. New taxes he continued to levy without cause, food he refused to distribute, borders he failed to protect, wars he'd started unprovoked—the list of his neglect stretched long and far.

At first, only a handful criticized Olok's rule, and they were quickly dismissed as fools with baseless accusations. Then, as the king's conduct grew even more suspect and oppressive, those who objected to the crown appeared in greater number. Now, those remaining loyal to the king became a precious minority.

As Captain of the King's Guard, Sir Lionel James was one of that minority. He had tried to see past the king's folly for as long as he could will himself, but now, he knew the man for what he truly was. Sir Lionel wanted nothing more than to abandon his post, but he had sworn an oath to protect and serve the king. He would not break the promise he'd made, even once he felt no sense of reverence, or even respect, for King Olok.

The city around the royal castle had been in turmoil for months, with assaults, theft, and murders by the score every day. The city guards were heavily pushed to their limits, and they had exhausted every last resource at their disposal in the fruitless attempt to maintain order. Three days ago, that turmoil brewed over into full rioting in the streets. The city guards who had not joined in the chaos had quickly been overrun by the mob. Olok commanded the military to the streets in an effort to quell the outbreak, but the soldiers who responded quickly were few in number and scarcely able to contain the madness. The military force required to subdue the mob was still two days away, and King Olok did not have two days to spare. The castle gates would be breached before the sun set that day.

Sir Lionel wondered where it had all gone awry. The knight searched his memory, trying to pinpoint the precise moment the king had lost his sense of honor. He did not know what unsettled him more—the possibility of having been oblivious to King Olok's descent into ruin, or the possibility of Olok never having been a proper king from the beginning. Sir Lionel had spoken to him on many occasions, and Olok never gave the impression of being a wicked man. The king's words were always kind and reassuring, clearly from an orator of some skill. It struck at Sir Lionel's core that a man's words and a man's deeds could so vastly differ in quality. Now, the miserable guilt over having willingly pledged his life and his loyalty to such a man plagued him.

The throne room of King Olok's castle seemed the last bastion of safety in the city. The screams of the mob could be heard from within the chamber, but the tangible presence of the riots were not felt within the room's walls. Sir Lionel had walked the lower halls of the castle, and they seemed to tremble and quake with the violence drawing ever closer. Only the king and a few knights, sealed within the room, remained by his side. Queen Donella had been sequestered within her own chambers, and Sir Lionel had not seen her since the rioting broke out. Olok remained upon the throne—his throne—ever silent and unmoved, as if he simply waited for the horde of enraged citizens to suddenly disperse and return to their homes. Sir Lionel had long given up trying to fathom what kind of thoughts filled the king's head.

Sir Lionel looked about the throne room and took stock of the men he commanded. They were all still honorable knights and loyal—if not loyal to the king, then at least to Sir Lionel. He knew he could count on his men to hold their ground when the time came.

The throne room was a defensible location; the architectural minds who had conceptualized the castle must have had a feel for war craft, if not some formal training. Only one main entrance led to a narrow path, funneling into the main chamber. That path could be filled and blocked by eight men standing shoulder-to-shoulder, and even with the dwindling number of knights at his call, Sir Lionel would be able to hold the passage with two full ranks. They would have no difficulty digging in and remaining entrenched in that corridor for hours, at the very least, against any attacker.

Clearly, the throne room would inevitably fall if support from the military did not show up very soon. If the time came to abandon the room, another passage existed, leading from the chamber to the catacombs beneath the castle. Well-secluded, that passage was only known to the Royal Family and Sir Lionel. The hidden escape was not even documented on the castle designs, charts, or maps. Sir Lionel could fall back with the king and slip out of the city, and from that point they could find a place to regroup and attempt to reestablish the crown. Even still, Sir Lionel wondered where in the world they would find friendly ground. King Olok had done little in the way of securing allies with whom they might find refuge.

Lionel searched desperately for ways the monarchy could survive this uprising. It seemed such a bitter end for a bloodline which had built a kingdom from nothing, though the knight knew well that all kings rose and fell over time. The adage had been impressed upon and accepted by many in the service of royalty, but it was never easy to reconcile when it was time for one's own king to fall. Perhaps the greatest tragedy of this monarchy was that it was not conquered by some greater nation, but instead fell beneath its own crushing weight. There would have been more honor in losing the throne to better men and braver warriors, but having it razed to ash by the poor and starving was yet another momentous black mark upon its legacy.

Sir Lionel turned his eye towards the king. Olok had been so withdrawn recently, as though the man had no care to save his kingdom or its people. Like a ship's captain solemnly clutching the helm of a sinking vessel, the king remained upon his throne in silence. The knight could not abide that silence any longer, nor could he in good conscience hold his own tongue if it might stem the tides of discord.

"Your Majesty, may we speak?" he asked, shifting uncomfortably in his chainmail. He strove to observe the finer points of etiquette when he could, diligent in refraining from addressing his betters until they spoke first, but the present circumstances were exceptional.

"You may say what you will, Sir Lionel," King Olok said, his voice distant and cold. When the king spoke, it sounded as though he had just wakened from a deep sleep, holding himself like a man who could not be bothered with the present.

"There may still be a way to quell the people's unrest and restore peace, Your Majesty." Sir Lionel felt fear creeping into his belly as he spoke. The knight knew he would have to overstep some boundaries of propriety, speaking now with the king, and that never sat well with him.

"By all means, elaborate. Tell me what you think will stop this insurrection." The king spoke with the voice of a cynic. He pouted his lips and rested his chin on a fist, looking at the Captain of the

Guard with all the indicators of a man unreceptive to any suggestion.

"Your subjects are starving. They have been taxed beyond their means. The coffers of the royal treasury are full enough. Perhaps some leniency is not out of the question. The people will behave peaceably if they are given some sign of mercy," Sir Lionel stated. It took much of his courage to speak the words, and he heard hushed expressions of disbelief and surprise from the knights he commanded as they listened to his address. It seemed as though this one man spoke aloud the thoughts of many in the room who had no resolve to speak it themselves.

"Give the mob what they demand. That is how you advise me?" Olok scoffed. "Give in to lawlessness and the demands of my subordinates? And for what? Nothing in return save the obedience to which I am already entitled. This is a fool's notion."

"The people need compassion," Lionel continued, trying to make his words sound as convincing as possible. "They will respect a gentle and kind king as much as they would laud a warlord. You would not be seen as weak were you to forgive the conduct of your subjects."

"All you need to do is hold the castle until my brother Duran brings the full might of my armies to this city," Olok said. "Then I will have order restored, and the people will see how merciful I am when I only execute *some* of them for treason. With fewer mouths to feed, there will be less starving."

Sir Lionel tried to think of some approach which might have an impact on the king, but it appeared the man remained beyond reason. The tension in the throne room ran high, but the focus of that tension rapidly shifted from the king and the captain of his guard to the sounds of the mob closing in as they stormed the castle.

The castle gates had fallen, and now the halls of the keep filled with fighting. The mob would soon reach the throne room, and Sir Lionel did not know how he would handle the coming battle. His head was not in this fight, nor was his spirit. It was all senseless. The

King could have prevented the realm from falling into such harsh circumstances but instead had chosen to let it all come to a fiery end.

Sir Lionel had not balked from the war in the mountains to the north which had taken ten years of his life. Then, it had been about serving king and country. Now, the war in which he was a part seemed fueled by neglect and oppression. More importantly, he felt he fought for the wrong side of this conflict. He saw none of the eight knightly virtues reflected in the king's desire to bring his people to heel. The knight touched the Blackstar embroidered on his tabard. It was the king's star, the star representing all that was good, and now Sir Lionel felt shame for wearing it.

A crash came at the throne room doors, and all eyes fixed upon the massive wooden bar holding them shut. Another crash, followed by another—the door would not hold much longer at all. The cracking of wood echoed off the stone walls as the bar that began to give, the doors swelling inward with each blow of the battering ram on the other side. The thick, broad hinges suddenly shook loose from where they had been anchored, deep into the castle's stone. Sir Lionel heard the mob's furious shouting and the curses they hurled at the king and the crown through the splintered doors—those doors now barely hung on their frame.

"Make ready!" Sir Lionel commanded. He took his place at the center of the front rank of the King's Guard. The knights on his flanks had longswords drawn and their shields fronted. The knights in the second rank held long spears firmly in their gauntleted hands. "Protect the king, protect the crown, protect the throne. We will stand and hold this hall. This is Loyalty right here," he continued.

The knight felt the word 'Loyalty' pass from his lips and knew the word should have come from genuine passion, but now, he only spoke out of duty. He felt as though he were slipping from the truth when he felt no fervor for what he spoke. He gave a small, backwards glance to see the king, who only sat upon his throne, dauntless and haughty as though nothing could dare touch him. Sir

Lionel was disgusted to his very core. What was about to happen was not the calling of a knight, nor of any man who cared for the eight virtues.

This was enough. Sir Lionel had killed enough good men in the name of the king and he could no longer stomach the act. He saw the faces of the people through the widening gaps in the doors—dirty, bloody, and above all, afraid. These were not warriors, and Sir Lionel would not put his steel to a people who simply wished not to starve.

"Hold!" Sir Lionel ordered his men. His knights stood easy but with varied glances of confusion shared amongst themselves. "No more of the kingdom's subjects will die here today. We shall stand down and retreat," he continued.

"What is this defiance? I say you will hold this hall and fight these peasants! I command you. Your king commands you!" Olok shouted. The doors were scarcely more than kindling and would be breached at any moment. Only wrath waited for them on the other side.

"Take the men to the left corner of the room behind the throne." Sir Lionel spoke quietly to Sir Altorn, the knight standing at his right hand. "There is a small passageway kept from view. It will lead you to the catacombs."

"But, Sir, the King," Altorn said with a complete lack of understanding.

Sir Lionel met the gaze of his brother knight and held it with guilty eyes before he turned and addressed Olok. "Our king commands us?" It was a bold start, and he chose to fuel it with mockery. "A king is a leader, a peacemaker, a compassionate servant of his people. I will obey the commands of my king without question. It is my honor to do so. But I will no longer obey your orders." He pointed an accusatory finger at Olok. "Because you are no king. You are a tyrant in a crown."

Most of the men in the room only responded with wide eyes

and gaping mouths. The outburst had shocked everyone, and time seemed to stand still in that moment. They had always known that what Sir Lionel had said was the truth, but now he had made it real for everyone by voicing it.

"Any man who wishes to stay, I will think no less of you. I can respect that loyalty. But I am leaving. I will no longer live this farce," he said. He looked to the rest of the guard and could tell by their faces that they were relieved someone else had taken the plunge first. None of them would fight for Olok any longer; this was plain to see.

"You swore an oath. You swore to me, to uphold my star. You swore on your steel," Olok raged as he pointed to the eight-pointed Blackstar on Sir Lionel's chest.

"I did swear an oath on steel. I swore to uphold the eight virtues of Honor, Loyalty, Chivalry, Commitment, Truth, Justice, Faith, and Tenacity. I swore to bring harmony to the realm. I did swear to serve and protect you, as well. Now, my oath is in conflict with itself. It is now an oath I must break to keep." Sir Lionel choked, gripping his longsword tightly with both hands. "Upholding the king's star also means holding the king accountable to it." Sir Lionel gritted his teeth and swung his sword. The knight struck the wall of the throne room with the flat of his blade, filling the space with the sound of breaking steel as his sword snapped in half.

"Now my oath to you is as the steel upon which it was sworn."

The rest of the king's guards let their own blades clatter to the ground, then hastily filtered from the room just as the doors were finally smashed to pieces. Sir Lionel was the last to reach the passage to the catacombs, just ahead of Olok as the man desperately fled from the tide of his vengeful subjects. After passing through the gate, Sir Lionel unhinged the portcullis chain separating the passage from the throne room, and the gate crashed to the floor. Olok was trapped on the wrong side.

"You will answer to your people. You will answer to the eight points of this star." Sir Lionel pointed to the Blackstar upon his tabard as he watched the mob set upon the man who had been their king. The tormented screams of the man the knight had once served echoed down the passage as Sir Lionel descended into the catacombs.

For Sir Lionel James, today would be that day.

"Soon, his spirit will part from the realm of man. His end will be tragic, unjustly so for one who has lived such as he. To have witnessed his striving for that which is good and righteous in his deeds and words lifted my heart to such heights. Upon his parting from the world below, I would see him counted among we who dwell in Paradise. Yet his heart bears a heavy burden of guilt, and for all his magnificent courage, fear has taken seed in his spirit. I hope upon my shield that my wings carry me swiftly to his side, swifter than the Reaper sure to come for him."

—Laurel, ArchValkyrie of the Thorn Crown

Broken Steel, Broken Words

Part 3

It was absolutely bizarre. He was about to die, and he spent his final moments attempting to recall the last thing he had eaten.

Sir Lionel James had been cut to ribbons. He sported wounds from head to toe, inflicted by sword, arrow, spear, and every other manner of weaponry. Even a heavy lance had contributed a gnarled gash across the knight's left thigh. His black and white tabard was a bloody ruin, barely managing to cling to his shredded chainmail. Still, the man drew breath and had strength left in his arms to hold his sword and shield.

Sir Lionel fought on in the face of mortal injury, and in that moment, the only thing to occupy his mind remained whether his breakfast had been porridge or eggs. Perhaps even more curious was the fact that the knight had always had a keen memory and now could not recall something that had happened less than a day ago. He knew, on some level, that this mental fog meant he was not long for this world. He had suffered many a grave injury in service of his king, his oath to protect the people and uphold the eight virtues, but he had always recovered from those wounds. Now, the knight knew that, once he fell today, he would rise no more.

Sir Lionel had not thought of what might happen after he'd abandoned King Olok's side. The knight had known it was the right thing to do, however seemingly contrary to an oath sworn. The difficulty for him lay in the fact that he had never envisioned his life beyond the king's star. In a single breath, so much of what Sir Lionel used to identify himself, to know his place and his purpose, had been lost.

Within three days of the king's death, Olok's younger brother Duran had learned Sir Lionel's hand itself had sealed the king's end at the wrath of an angry mob. Duran had condemned Sir Lionel as an Oath Breaker. Duran still held the highest command in the Royal Army and dispatched every soldier, wagon, and horse under his control to hunt down and kill the man whose cowardice and dishonor simultaneously ended the life and reign of the nation's good King Olok.

Nothing but bloody days followed for Sir Lionel and what remained of the King's Guard. He had made it clear that any man who had worn the Blackstar of the King's Guard remained under no obligation to follow his leadership any longer. He had told them they were all free to disburse, to try to build some kind of lives for themselves beyond the black and white and beyond the eight-pointed star. Even though everyone understood the Captain's words, none abandoned Sir Lionel. Even when he impressed upon them that those who continued to follow him would likely also be condemned as treasonous Oath Breakers, his men remained loyal. To a man, and for better or worse, they all vowed to share in whatever fate befell Sir Lionel. The knights knew continued loyalty would likely be a death sentence, but they would not abandon the one man who had brought a faint glimmer of nobility and righteousness to the end of King Olok's rule.

Duran had little difficulty in locating Sir Lionel and his Oath Breakers. They were the most notorious men in the kingdom, after all. The knights had scarce allies to call upon, and finding even remotely hospitable shelter for a single evening challenged them. The rebellion in the city around Olok's castle had been crushed as soon as Duran returned with the might of the Royal Army. For those rebellious subjects who survived the initial return of Duran's force, only gruesome executions awaited them.

While many of the kingdom's people continued to nurture animosity towards the crown in their hearts, few were so outspoken about it when word spread of the fate meted out to those in the royal city. The remnants of the royal family harbored a formidable, wild rage. Most people would not further cultivate the risk of being branded a usurper by actually supporting a known enemy to take the crown. Duran did not have to offer any reward for knowledge of Sir Lionel and his men. The kingdom's people were only too eager to direct the Royal Army in the pursuit of the traitorous knight, especially if it meant their families would be spared a beating and their homes spared from fire. The people once again lived in dread and would to anything to see such a heavy weight lifted.

Day after day, Sir Lionel and his Oath Breaker Knights fled, the Royal Army close at their heels. It was a hopeless effort, for the knights had no place to run and no place to hide. The already minute contingent of men following Sir Lionel grew hastily smaller as one Oath Breaker after another fell to the Royal Army. Each time Duran came within reach, Sir Lionel evaded capture for just a little longer, often at the expense of one or more of his brother knights.

Now, there was nowhere left to go. Sir Lionel and the three men remaining at his side had been pushed all the way to the rocky cliffs of the kingdom's coast. They found fleeting refuge in an abandoned watchtower, sitting high on a windy bluff and overlooking the unending cascade of ocean waves to the east. They managed to find one final night of rest and fellowship, safe, warm, and dry within the crumbling stones of the watchtower before breaking their fast on what they knew would be their final morning.

The Royal Army had been spotted from the top of the watchtower parapets as the sun rose. Armored men in numbers beyond counting approached the rickety structure, and Sir Lionel and the last of the King's Guard silently watched the advance of those who heralded their impending deaths. It was more than intimidating to see a tide of soldiers descend upon the watchtower, but the four knights steeled themselves and pushed fear from their spirits.

At the vanguard of the Royal Army was Duran himself, sitting astride a jet-black horse. The late king's younger brother looked as though he had already claimed victory and was most certainly enjoying this moment. *Unwarranted pride and arrogance must be family traits*, thought Sir Lionel as he watched Duran shout commands at his men, waving his arms about in a grand spectacle.

The Royal Army had fast pinned the watchtower between an ocean of freezing blue water and a sea of well-armed, fighting men. There was no place left for the four Oath Breakers to fall back, and this derelict watchtower would undoubtedly be the knights' tomb. Death was a certainty, but their lives would not be so easily stolen. The steep, sloping terrain of the coast meant that catapults, trebuchets, and any other larger war machines could not advance on the location of Sir Lionel's final stand. The hills and grassy knolls of the kingdom's coastline were formidable enough, and it even proved difficult for the Royal Army to maneuver wagon and horse or to march in formation.

The watchtower may have been long forgotten and uncared for, but its stones were still broad and sound. A far cry from an impenetrable fortress, the single spiral staircase would provide a strong defense against the insurmountable number of soldiers coming for Sir Lionel. As long as the knights remained in the stairwell below the parapets, they would be safe from Duran's archers. This way, the army could only send in a few men at a time, at equal numbers to the remaining knights and at close combat. Man-to-man and blade-to-blade, the black and white knights wearing the eight-pointed star were deadliest. Duran would claim the lives of the Oath Breakers, but the effort would cost him dearly.

Sir Lionel felt a pit in his stomach when he saw the Royal Army halt their advance. He realized that, while his men held a reasonably defensible location, Duran could simply starve them out. With the lack of drink alone, the four knights would be dead within seven days' time. But the fear of such an end quickly dissolved when he saw the ranks of men outside the watchtower shift and prepare to launch an attack. As sure a death as patience would provide, Duran no doubt wanted to capture Sir Lionel alive, if at all possible, to then whisk him away to the hands of the Master Inquisitor and the castle dungeon's assorted torture devices.

"I am ready. It is my privilege to fight beside men of your quality," Sir Lionel said to the last of the King's Guard. All three knights nodded in acknowledgment, and in unison the four men spoke. "Honor, Loyalty, Chivalry, Commitment, Truth, Justice, Faith, Tenacity". They touched the Blackstar upon their tabards, then drew swords and readied shields.

It was a grueling combat without end. The four Oath Breakers held the base of the watchtower against impossible odds. They were pushed back onto the winding stairwell twice by the Royal Army, but both times, Sir Lionel and his men fought their way back to the entranceway below. While the base of the watchtower was not as well-protected as the thick stones of the stairwell, Lionel knew it was important to hold as much ground as he could at the onset of battle. He would need every step of that stairwell to fall back upon and would not freely give up any distance to the enemy. Once the Oath Breakers were forced to the top of the watchtower, they would receive a rain of arrows from archers at the foot of the building, and it would all be over.

The Royal Army's men were trained soldiers, but they were no match for the knights they fought while the weight of their numbers were not at their advantage. Nearing midday, the tides of infantry had been turned back again and again, so Duran ordered two cavalry charges on the position. The maneuvers bore the Royal Army little fruit beyond a wound on Sir Lionel's leg. The cavalry charges, like each wave of infantry commanded to advance, had cost the lives of every soldier sent.

Fatigue had long set in on Sir Lionel and his men. The exhaustion the Oath Breakers felt with each swing of their swords was titanic; even keeping their shields at the ready was no longer a small task. That fatigue, coupled with the numerous superficial wounds the knights sustained, ultimately led to Sir Cedrick missing a parry and finding a footman's mace caving his forehead into a broken, wet mush. This loss meant the knights could no longer rotate two frontline fighters evenly while the other two took moments to rest. They were forced onto the watchtower's stairwell yet again, but this time, they could not push back the forces of the Royal Army.

The narrow confines of the watchtower stairwell utterly nullified the advantage of numbers for the Royal Army. It was difficult for even two men to stand side by side along the twisting path. Inside the stone walls, Sir Lionel and his last two knights fought with renewed zeal. Duran lost man after man to the Oath Breakers; the knights possessed skill and endurance far beyond the capability of the Royal Army soldiers when faced in single combat. The day stretched on, and Sir Lionel and his men continued to rotate, two of the three standing to fight while the third rested on the steps behind them.

The defiance of these three men infuriated Duran, and his officers and command staff gave the late king's younger brother a wide birth to vent his frustrations. The battle had stopped a full four times so the Royal Army could send men into the watchtower to remove the dead, dying, and wounded soldiers filling the stairwell and hindering the Army's press for ground. Duran ordered the bulk of his men to fall back out of sight, claiming it was a tactical ploy to try luring Sir Lionel out to open ground. But the truth was simply that he wanted to cull the evident demoralization of his men as they were subjected to an unending parade of their dead and maimed comrades removed from the watchtower.

Eventually, the insurmountable number of men at Duran's disposal took its toll on those who stood against him. The Oath Breakers only continued to lose ground as the plethora of minor wounds they each suffered grew and compounded. The watchtower steps ran slick with blood of men from both sides.

Sir Lionel rested in the fighting rotation. He had been pushed so far back up the watchtower stairs that he could see daylight above. Any more ground lost to the Royal Army meant the archers below could take aim and loose arrows with deadly intent. He was just about to switch places and rejoin the fight when the inevitable finally happened.

Sir Michael lost the grip on his blade and it clattered to the stone steps at his feet. An instant later, a sword cleaved into the right side of the man's head and killed him on impact. Sir Jonathon soon followed his brother knight into death when a soldier's axe collapsed his ribs, and several swords then found their mark in his chest.

Now it was only Sir Lionel—one man against an army. The Oath Breaker knight fought with all his remaining strength, but it was far too little for the task before him. He held his position on the top steps for as long as he could, but Duran's soldiers quickly forced the lone man onto the watchtower's open parapets. Still, he fought his attackers.

The top of the watchtower was far more open than the narrow stairwell below, and Sir Lionel backed himself into a corner to keep from being surrounded. He struck blow after blow, his sword finding shield, armor, flesh. The combat only endured for a moment before the solders of the Royal Army consolidated in the mouth of the stairwell and locked their shields tight, trapping Sir Lionel on the exposed platform. He waited for what he knew was coming.

"Bowmen, lose!" came the call from the base of the watchtower. The telltale snap of many bowstrings and the whir of ranged weapons followed. Sir Lionel raised his battered, warped shield to protect his head and chest as best as he could. The arrow shafts poured down atop the watchtower, many of them clanging off his shield, but there were just too many to defend himself. The knight felt the sting of sharpened metal rip into the muscles of his legs. He had no strength left in his body, and his shield clattered to the ground, where several arrows struck the man in the chest and cast him over the side of the watchtower.

He fell far and fast. The dying knight plummeted down the cliff side towards the waves crashing on rocks beneath. He looked to the sky as he rapidly descended. Among the clouds the knight saw the strangest thing—the form of a woman of indescribable beauty. Her skin was alabaster white and flawless, her eyes as blue as an unclouded sky. She was clad in brilliant armor of silver and gold, and from her back extended two massive, blazing-white feathered wings. The woman reached out her hand and flew toward Sir Lionel as he fell through the air.

"Take my hand, brave knight, and know peace and joy," her voice rang inside his mind.

Sir Lionel stretched out his hand toward hers. He felt warmth and calm replace the pain running through his body. The woman flew fast and faster toward the knight. His vision, which had begun to fade into darkness, filled with a beautiful white light. She was only a stone's throw from his fingertips now; she would catch him before he fell into the ocean below. Sir Lionel felt his heart lighten and serenity take hold of his being, so warm and peaceful. Then, in a moment, the women's utter beauty transformed into a face etched with dismay and terror.

From the churning and frothing water below, the Reaper exploded in a torrent of blackness and anguish. Its long, tattered black cloak whipped in the wind as it snatched Sir Lionel from the air. The Reaper clutched the knight to its breast with freezing arms of shadow and nightmare. The warmth and peace which had filled Sir Lionel vanished, replaced with only cold—cold beyond cold. Sir Lionel saw tears mark the face of the white-winged woman as the Reaper pulled him away from her outstretched hand.

"Now you belong to Death, Oath Breaker," hissed the Reaper with a voice forged from sorrow and grief.

The Reaper pulled the knight beneath the waves, bringing him down. It brought him down to darkness and ice, to a realm beyond hope. It brought him down to a land filled with demons and monsters, a place of unending torment. It brought him down to nothing but weeping and the gnashing of teeth.

It brought him to Purgatory.

Epilogue

Cold—cold beyond cold. The cold was the first thing of which the knight became aware. Sir Lionel James felt the freeze of icy water running over his body before he noticed anything else. His eyes opened, and the things he saw—oh, the things he saw!

He was washed up on a bank of jagged black rocks, formed of a mineral with a glassy, reflective sheen and a scent to them like smoke. The knight looked inland as far as the water's glow would illuminate. He saw trace movements of shadowy things waiting beyond the places where the water's dim light repelled the darkness. He was not alone in this place.

Sir Lionel's legs were still fully submerged in the tides rolling in and out from the shore. The water chilling his bones could not rightly be called water; indeed, it was liquid, but a deathly pale, sickly green hue, emanating a sinister glow. Sir Lionel looked past his legs and saw neither shore in the distance nor any sign of an end to the currents which had washed him there. The knight viewed strange, ghostly apparitions, swirling and frothing just below the water's surface. They moved in an unnatural fashion and seemed to have a measure of consciousness—a self-awareness about them as they slithered through the pale, green glow.

He looked above into a gargantuan black void. There were no stars in the sky, but then the knight realized he did not gaze upon the sky. It felt like some sort of ceiling for the place, like a cave or cavern and not a beach or riverbank at all. Then he noticed the feel of the air around him, hanging heavy and without any trace of wind or the slightest breeze. The air in this place was not fresh but thick, rank, and clung to the skin, filling Sir Lionel's nostrils with the odor of rot and decay. The knight had to forcibly stop himself from retching and choking on the putrid taste of soot and ash filling his mouth. No, this place was not open to the sky.

More than the vision of the grotesque and infinite spectral sea, more than the noxious smell of all things dead, more than the numbing cold permeating everything and the stomach-curdling taste that could not be washed away, the sounds of this place haunted him most. Screams of terror, cries of pain, the sobbing of hopelessness—all filled this place with a cacophony of torment and suffering. Past the edge of total darkness, Sir Lionel heard sounds born of nightmares—serpentine hissing and guttural howls of things not human from beyond the black shroud of eternal night.

After the initial overwhelming of his senses as he woke to this frightening new world, Sir Lionel became more conscious of himself. He remembered fleeing the castle before it was overrun by the mob. He remembered the battle at the watchtower. He remembered the innumerable wounds he suffered in that fight and then the fall from the cliff. He remembered being in pain, his brother knights dying at his side.

He remembered dying.

Sir Lionel did not feel the pain which had riddled his body before he woke to this new place; where the pain had once been, now he felt only numbness and cold. He rolled from his belly and sat up, looking his body over and stunned to see no wounds, no blood, no dirt or grime. His armor and tabard had been fully restored. The knight's shield lay on the bank beside him, unmarred. Sir Lionel was whole once again.

His attention was caught by an image within the sickly tides in which he remained mired. It was his reflection cast in the water, and he knew it was his reflection though he did not fully recognize his face. His visage was now somehow reminiscent of a corpse, cheeks gaunt and eyes sunken, and the knight removed one of his leather gloves to note the complexion of his skin; it was now the same deathly pale shade of the water before him. Sir Lionel touched his face with his boney hands and felt the sting of winter's frost beneath his fingertips. *What have I become?* he thought.

"Get out of the water, now!" came a shout from his right. The knight turned his head to find the source of the voice and saw what appeared to be a man running along the rocky bank towards him. He then felt something take hold of his heels with great force, pulling him back into the water. He scrambled to find purchase upon the jagged, glossy stones, but the rocks crumbled to dust wherever his hands bore down.

Sir Lionel was pulled chest-deep back into the pale, glowing tide by one of the swirling specters beneath its surface, and the knight drew the dagger sheathed at his waist to drive its point into the black rock as far as he could. This only gave a few moments' pause from descent into the watery depths before chunks of the sable rock broke free and Sir Lionel's dagger came loose.

The glowing water closed over his head and filled his nose and mouth with its bitter, cold kiss. Sir Lionel thrashed about wildly, trying to find some way to extract himself from the water. He broke the surface, and his ears met a sound like the crack of thunder coming from the shore. The knight was tugged below the water once again. He felt something take hold of his hand and pull him towards the bank, then he thrust his other hand towards the shore and felt something grip that, too. With the arrival of an ally on the shore, the attacking phantom released its clutches on the man.

The knight was pulled from below the water and found himself standing safe on solid ground. The man who had shouted a warning stood before the knight. He was an older man, clad in garb to which Sir Lionel was unaccustomed, though his dress seemed finely crafted of cloth and tanned leather. The wispy hair trailing from beneath his brown leather cap was more silver than brown, as was his mustache.

The man who had saved Sir Lionel had a hauntingly deep gaze, holding within it both a warrior's resolve and a gentle kindness. But the man's most striking features were those similar to Lionel's own—the sickly pale skin, eyes sunken back into their sockets, and the cheekbones of someone who had not had a meal for some time.

"My gratitude for your chivalry, brave sir. I am Sir Lionel James, Knight of the Realm and formerly Captain of the King's Guard." It took him a few moments after his ordeal in the water to regain his composure enough to speak.

"Yer welcome, son. Are you all right, there?" the man asked as he looked over the knight with a stare belying surprise and bewilderment. Clearly, Sir Lionel appeared as foreign to his rescuer as the man seemed to him.

"May I have the honor of your name?" Sir Lionel asked.

"I'm Marshal Jackson Bennett French," said the man.

About the Author

Photo by Leah Sharae Photography

Jason Pere is a born-and-raised New Englander. He always had a passion for the arts and creative storytelling. At the age of thirteen, Jason took up the craft of acting for film and theater. He pursued that interest for over a decade until refocusing his medium of expression into writing.

At first, Jason took a causal interest in writing, starting with poetry and journaling. Over time, he honed his direction and finally began writing larger works. In November of 2012, Jason self-published his first book, *Modern Knighthood: Diary of a Warrior Poet.*

Since then, Jason has continued writing on his own, mostly short stories and poetry. *Calling the Reaper* was his first experience committing to a full-length Fiction title.

In early 2015, Jason became affiliated with Collaborative Writing Challenge (CWC). Since then, he has joined many other writers on numerous collaborative projects. Jason is a regular contributor to CWC and is scheduled to have multiple pieces of his work appear in their publications.

You can find out more about Jason Pere's involvement in collaborative fiction at:

www.collaborativewritingchallenge.com

Thank you so much for taking the time to read Calling the Reaper. If you enjoyed it, please don't forget to leave a review at your favorite retailer and let us know what you thought.

Jason Pere

https://www.facebook.com/jbp.author/
http://teamcovenant.com/category/ashes-rise-of-the-phoenixborn
jbp.author@gmail.com